THE LABOURS OF CHARLES E.

Cb

Other Books by Ian Gouge

Novels and Novellas

The Red Tie
17 Alma Road
Tilt
Once Significant Others
On Parliament Hill
A Pattern of Sorts
The Opposite of Remembering
At Maunston Quay
An Infinity of Mirrors
The Big Frog Theory
Losing Moby Dick and Other Stories

Short Stories

Dust, dancing
An Irregular Piece of Sky
Degrees of Separation
Secrets & Wisdom

Poetry

Less
Bound
Grimsby Docks
Crash
not the Sonnets
Selected Poems: 1976-2022
The Homelessness of a Child
The Myths of Native Trees
First-time Visions of Earth from Space
After the Rehearsals
Punctuations from History
Human Archaeology
Collected Poems (1979-2016)

Non-Fiction

So, you think you're a Writer
Shrapnel from a Writing Life

Ian Gouge

The Labours of Charles E.

Devils

1949 - 1967

Did you scream as he took you?

Or did you lay there passive — knowing he was too strong — and wait for it to be over?

And later, to try and wash away the stream of his violation, hoping nothing would come of it, perhaps wishing it had been gifted to you by someone else. Gently.

Or was part of you thrilled by the unspeakable passion of it, such an extreme departure from your sheltered upbringing. So out of character, like Deborah Kerr surrendering on the beach.

Have I always wanted to know what it was like for you? Even though I wasn't yet there. Even though *I* was the outcome. Or *we* were the outcome, Matthew and me.

Perhaps my desire to understand has nothing to do with facts, however they might have been pieced together over time. There was always so little from you, nothing to be mined from your reluctance to talk. Later, hearsay would offer glimpses, as would reportage, internet searching in times much closer to now. Yet if I was seeking something other than a factual understanding, in what medium might that be found? In how you felt, I suppose; I mean, how you *really* felt. And how you responded, then, later, forever after.

Have I always been fascinated by your scars?

I wonder if they were genetically shared between the three of us.

Or was it more a matter of my wanting ownership, possession? To feel I had endured something not dissimilar to you and could therefore comprehend, look back on life from

"

other vantage points and surface other events, my own scarring? Perhaps ultimately it might have been no more than the search for kinship — if only from one brutal incident.

You were the victim, clearly; a kind of Eve, subjugated to the serpent which spawned so much else. Helpless, I assume you were; unable to find a way out — which is ironic given you'd managed to find a way in. Into his life and into his bed (if that's where the climactic deed took place). And then out of both even more quickly.

There is a kind of melodrama to be imagined; yet even so, I cannot see you as the victim who would go running down the street, yelling in anguish, screaming at the world. That was not your style. Not in public anyway. Nor in my memory of you.

Now unable to ask, I would still like to know whether you thought time was eventually kind to you, collaborating in the blurring of memory. As much as such a thing could be erased, that is. I want to imagine you forgiven by time, offered a means to attain peace and to relegate the memory of your rape to somewhere else, somewhere distant, obscured from your view. While in my own case — seeing as how it was the *beginning* of things, the beginning of *me* — how could I not continually strive for greater focus, greater understanding, even across a distance of so many years?

My calendar continually reminds me of time's passing. Each year I see the span between now and when he did what he did grow incrementally; just as life's stock of unanswered questions grows. Counter-intuitively, even after the gifting of wisdom (no more than a sleight of hand?) time remorselessly continues to pile its myriad of uncertainties upon me. It is as if *I* have yet to be forgiven, as if *I* need to take responsibility, to reimagine — even to re-experience as best I might. But via narratives constructed from a safe distance. Obviously.

And with that 'journey' (for want of a better term), comes something else, something unrelated to conception and birth. Or even living, to a degree. It is a weighing, a passing of judgement.

Not on you — even if there was once a time when I might have wanted to set the scales myself. Or more than one time, if I'm honest. Because without what happened (whether you were victim or not) I would never have been required to suffer, to weigh, to choose and calculate, to make my own mistakes.

And to judge.

Victim or perpetrator? In some senses I think there is little difference, especially across a chasm of more than three-score-years-and-ten. And given my own history, I have to believe that such ambivalence is vital if only for sanity's sake. Yet are our histories not merely two sides of the same coin; a coin which now requires its alloy to be tested for purity — or imperfections — whether I want such assaying to be carried out or not.

Apparently.

~

Was it abandonment, your immediately giving us up? The cold-hearted replication of what he did to you, the clock moved on less than a year? If so, it was a harsh lesson to be taught. And so much later — after being reunited — had we been expecting an apology, whispered in a quiet moment perhaps as reward for reaching our teenage years, we were to be disappointed. Then later still, more strenuously pressed (if only by me), you claimed what you'd done — abandoned us — had been 'right', as if unavoidably adhering to some irrefutable universal law.

What choice did I have? you said, playing your victim card as you would the ace of trumps in a game of whist, the first adult game you taught us — and one you used to let us win until you couldn't prevent us from condemning you to defeat.

How did you feel about that? Not the losing at cards, but giving up your children, choice and 'right' notwithstanding? Again you never said, not even when we were old enough to have begun to understand. And later, when it was suddenly too late for Matthew, did you also view his absence as abandonment — though this time of you, the second side of another coin? If so, it was a coin I would flip myself soon enough.

Whether at the start of things or the end — or at any point in between — you couldn't possibly have known what was to come next.

But in those first postpartum days, what else was to be done but to place trust in a formal body, a process, anonymous others. It would have been a handing-over without ceremony or fanfare; the physical exchange of twins a few days old, requiring nothing more than the turning of your back and looking away. Metaphorical and actual? Filled with regret? Remorse or relief? Was that the beginning or the end of your life? How did you see it?

And for us? We couldn't have known you then; we who weren't introduced to you until much later when — your role almost inexplicably reversed — you arrived in our lives like a saviour, gathering us up. It was perhaps another beginning. Who is to judge? Not you, not now. Perhaps that is my role: judge and jury. And executioner? But no; that would be inadequate and superficial. Maybe I should be passing sentence on myself too... And what about the others, the roles they played in our journey between the spark and when it really all began?

Like Martha O'Connell and her weak lily-livered husband Timothy. Initially, she would have presented well I'm sure: solid, respectable, and — leaning on her Irish Catholic upbringing — claiming all the virtues to be gleaned from supposed faith. And Timothy (she would have argued) had a good job, was conscientious, loyal. If an interview of sorts, I doubt you would have been in much of a state to conduct it. Perhaps it was executed elsewhere — and by those who should have been able to see through her blarney. I suspect all that was required of you was to acquiesce to the process. Job done. Pain followed by nine months of turmoil, followed by more pain; all swept away by the tip of a cheap ballpoint pen on some official document. Sign on the dotted line.

Just as we would then be swept away — babes-not-in-arms — into the clutches of the O'Connell's.

I assume there was some financial recompense due to them. Why else would Martha have taken on twins not much more than a few days old? Not out of a sense of compassion or fellow feeling, that much is now clear. In the seven years she owned us we saw no examples of that.

It took some time for me to piece her history together; but this happened much, much later, and never with you as an active contributor. There was a kind of distillation involved, a filtering of fact from fiction.

She was Irish, yes; but from lowly stock. She'd learned hard lessons on a farm and from a father who taught her parenting via the buckle-end of a strap. Arriving in England and soon snaring Timothy, Martha was a woman bent on revenge. Her whole reason for being had been twisted into vengeance — and in any way possible. Timothy was probably a decent enough chap. At least in the beginning. Indeed there were times (we were probably five or six) when he'd take us to the park and, for a few precious hours out of her sight, we three were almost like a normal family. Perhaps we were able to be precocious in those rare moments; children even. But to walk back under Martha O'Connell's roof was to see her husband transformed into something less than a man, and Matty and I into playthings. No, *less* than playthings. Rag dolls to be beaten and pummelled and thrown across the room.

Oh, she had her passions! Bullying, violence, dishonesty. She told Timothy she wanted children as desperately as he did; it was an excuse for as much rough sex as he could cope with, sex we heard through the thin walls of our shabby two-up, two-down. But she initiated their romping knowing she couldn't have any children of her own. I never knew why; something in her history? Was that where we'd come in? It was a lie which kept him in thrall. Perhaps he thought motherhood would change her, mellow her. If so, then he was truly blind to how she treated us. Or maybe his loyalty knew no bounds.

In all things she came first — and no-one came second. The three of us were also-rans, Timothy perhaps just above the gutter in which she was determined we wallow.

Sometimes Matty and I would count our bruises to see who had the most — and she made us wear long trousers and long-sleeved shirts to school so that no-one else could.

Why were we not rescued? Why wasn't the person who filed Martha's endorsed version of those same forms you signed not there for us? I vaguely recall official visits when she'd smarten the house up, put on make-up, her best dress, make Timothy wear his suit. And there'd be cake — and she'd warn us that if we acted up when 'the lady' came, she'd break our arms. Carrot and stick I suppose. But it was sufficient — tea and cake — to con someone from the council, someone who thought they had more important places to be. And it was the 1950s. No-one would have given a shit then anyway.

Odd how, in a way, I'm grateful to the old bitch. She taught me how to be resolute. By the time I was seven — by the time *we* met — I was already hardened; harder than Matty, that's for sure. I wasn't the baby you'd given up. Nor was I the child you might have raised. I'd become someone who'd learned about lies and telling stories and manipulation; I'd been watching a master at work.

And I knew about punishment too; what it looked like, the various ways it could be administered. I'm not proud of that, especially if later on I took advantage of that knowledge from time to time. In my own way.

We all have our scars.

~

Those last few days with her and Timothy in Portsmouth. Both normal and abnormal. Is it some aberration of hindsight that wants me to remember them as particularly hard, Martha excelling herself in terms of vindictiveness? I see Matty enduring fresh beatings, seeding the bruises that would soon bloom under your watchful gaze. But that may be no more than twisted remembrance. Another lie.

Even if it was true — Martha stepping up the brutality, Timothy retreating further into his shell — I'm sure we had no clue as to why. She would never have offered us any hope. 'Martha' and 'hope' never occurred in the same sentence — except perhaps this one.

Back from school that Friday afternoon, Timothy insisted we go and play football in the park. That was the first unusual thing. Had we known he had all our things packed into two suitcases in the back of his car... And so we played for a while. Then you and Jack, both strangers, appeared out of nowhere — along with that woman from the council who'd occasionally been to tea. We recognised her.

She sat us down on a bench and told us what was happening. Who you were. Who Jack was. Then I turned round, saw our cases resting on the path — and that Timothy had gone.

'Mother' was a new term for us. It was devoid of context. Of meaning almost. A word without a home. We'd never called

Martha mother; I'm not sure we would have done so even if she'd encouraged us to. What *did* we call her? You know, I don't think I can recall. But now — out of the blue — there was this stranger being introduced to us: our 'mother'. Someone to whom we could attach the traditional associations of the word, invest it with feelings and warmth.

We'd had no opportunity to be nervous, not as you had. Later you confessed as much. *I didn't sleep the night before*, you said, *and not much the night before that either*. And later still, *I did what I knew was right*. 'Right' again. Then, *Jack made it all possible*.

We played football with Jack for a bit while the council woman spoke to you. Youthful, enthusiastic, I liked him immediately, and when we finished playing we walked back to the bench with Matty holding his hand.

Another hand-over, I suppose.

And then it was the weekend. All that newness to get used to: new house, new bedrooms, new mealtimes. I heard Matty crying himself to sleep on the Sunday. I think he was worried it was all a dream and that Martha would be there again on Monday to pick us up from school, to resume the torture.

But she wasn't there then, nor on Tuesday, nor the rest of the week. It was the turning of a page, the beginning of a new chapter — metaphors that seem entirely appropriate given what was to follow between then and now. I mean, if I'm not qualified to use them then who is?

'Mum' and 'dad' you became soon enough. Especially for Matty.

You gave us various flavours of your story, most often settling on the fiction that you'd been unwell; that it had taken a long time for you to get better; that Martha was only supposed to be temporary. You were sorry, you said; but it was not a proper apology, rather some kind of glue intended to fix two pieces of your history together. A botch-job really. I don't think I truly believed any of it even then, though perhaps that says more about me than you.

If I was being generous — and knowing what I know now — I might allow you an illness of some persuasion, concede that what you had been through entitled you to recuperation. Mentally. Even at our expense. Especially as it was soon evident — and to a seven-year-old! — that Jack was *your* rescuer, the one who hauled you out of whatever abyss you had fallen into.

He had a certain rugged charm about him. Like Richard Burton in *The Desert Rats*. It was an easy parallel to draw given he'd fought in North Africa. His stories — filled with heroism and excitement, bravery and derring-do — were a world away from what we had become used to. For Matty, oblivious to their sugar-coating (deliberate or otherwise), they were just another reason to idolise him; yet for me his tales demonstrated different ways to lay out a story, to fabricate. As such they were part of my writerly education I suppose, Jack's stories. And yours too. If anything, I learned that truth was seldom to be found on the surface of things — and when it was, such truth often came with a whack, a thump, the purpleness of a bruise.

How quickly did we adapt? We were kids. Change came easy. By the end of that summer's holiday the transplant was complete, the rescue affected, the future re-written. As if I needed proof, at some point early that summer I remember seeing Matty get out of the bath and realised there wasn't a single bruise on him.

Protective of my own damage, I never talked about Martha, even when you asked me to.

~

If people other than you or our teachers made assumptions about us as twins — for how can I give credence to anything the O'Connell's may have thought? — I suspect they would have been lazy notions, fitting stereotypes. Isn't that the simplest way to frame people, to begin to judge them? But we two were very different.

Matty was the delicate, emotional one; the boy who yearned to be cuddled, loved; the boy who, just a few years later, feared he might be gay; the boy who craved to be told what he wanted to hear. Not what he needed to hear, mind. If you'd had sufficient cotton wool you would have wrapped him in it, you and Jack. Maybe you tried.

Is it any wonder I think Martha did more harm to him than me?

As much as I loved and wanted to protect him, there was always a weakness in him that angered me. I can confess that now. I tried not to bully him, not to take advantage, but sometimes refraining was impossible. Had you succeeding in wrapping him in that cotton wool, I think I might have occasionally torn it away, tried to force him to be something else, to 'man up'. An odd notion for a boy not yet an adult and with no idea what 'manning up' might mean.

And how was I? Another coin — or a different side.

I excelled at the physical things; was quicker, stronger. I was the one who helped Jack in the garden, the shed; the one who was better at football, faster at running; the son most likely to help carry shopping from the supermarket. You never said — no-one ever said — but all those attributes ended up labelling me, us: Matty, sensitive and bright; me, the brawny one.

Conclusions were drawn. Assumptions made.

But everyone was proved wrong, weren't they — even if I'm now desmonstrating that I'm not physically infallible.

Three years later — three years under your roof, your protection — the teachers told you that academically Matty would fly and I would falter. The 11-plus was to be the independent judge which would make the assessment, pass sentence. *After all*, someone said redundantly, *being a twin didn't necessarily lead to equality in everything.*

Matty passed as expected, but it proved a struggle for him, his grades were marginal. He'd allowed his emotions to get the better of him, that was what you decided; and the 'stress' story was a fable everyone was happy to buy into. He was delicate remember, he didn't handle pressure well; after all, he'd had such a difficult beginning. His time would come; he would flourish.

I watched the tale being woven that post-exam summer and kept my counsel. I never believed in Fairy Stories; how could I?

And me?

It was hard to know who was the most surprised — except that it wasn't me. Perhaps it was old Mr Whitehurst. I remember the meeting in school when he asked to see you, the three of us tucked into one corner of his classroom after everyone else had gone home, sitting on those little plastic chairs. *The highest marks in the year* he'd said, shaking his head not merely as if he couldn't believe it, but also in a kind of marvelled disappointment at everyone else. *And not only that, the best scores from anyone in the school, ever.*

I can't be sure if I smiled, though I suppose I must have. But I do recall the look of surprise, the shock on your face, as if there had been an error, some monumental cock-up. Surely they'd given me someone else's marks. Matty's probably.

Not only did you not understand what Whitehurst had told you, I think you'd struggled to comprehend what it might mean. Sage-like, he spelled it out for you. I remember that much. *If he works hard, makes the usual amount of progress, then university is a certainty.* But I don't think you understood what 'university' meant. I mean, why should you? And neither did

I, not then. All I knew was that I was the best; no longer just the fastest and strongest at home, but the 'best' in the school.

And I hadn't even tried.

In it's own way, it represented another beginning. A third start. And I was still only ten-years-old.

Don't waste it, Laddie Whitehurst said as we left him that afternoon. I had no idea what he meant, not then; but I'd like to be able to ask him now what he thought, how he would judge me sixty-five years on. Oddly, I think what he said would somehow matter.

But he's been long gone these last fifty years or so.

And he's not the only one who's left the stage.

~

You always asked so many questions. We thought it was because you didn't understand, not because you wanted to. And because Matty didn't, we assumed he knew already, that he was therefore the brighter one. But that wasn't the case, was it? He was just shy, or ashamed he couldn't see things the way you could. You were ashamed of nothing. We thought that was a sign too.

~

No matter how I tried, I was unable to take Whitehurst's advice. I didn't seem to need to. I breezed into the new school at eleven, then sauntered through that. Matty was diligent, worked hard; I just did enough to get by. And by 'get by' I mean I was always in the top two or three, good O-levels never in doubt. I played by the rules — except where I could get away with not doing so. Or where there were advantages in taking a risk. Overall the bar had been raised: the kids were bright enough, but even so I never felt they were any kind of threat, never a challenge.

Not until Stefan Hamer came to school.

A year above me, he arrived with whisperings about his ancestry, rumours he had Germanic roots. And we were still close enough to nineteen-forty-five for that to be relevant. True or not, it was a legend he was happy enough not to deny. The reputation he soon built for himself was as 'the bad boy of the school', a mantle he had no trouble carrying.

I met him through the football team. By then I was only an occasional player while he was one of the stars, a compact individual who played with an aggression beyond his years. Rumour had it he wanted to be a jockey — and that his father was a small-time crook. Later, I was to wonder whether Stefan wasn't also engaged in some kind of general vendetta, though against whom I wasn't sure. Perhaps everyone.

Within weeks of his arrival there were stories of him screwing at least one of the girls in my year — and that he'd been caught coming into school drunk one morning. I couldn't substantiate the first claim, but the second…

He introduced me to alcohol. Initially it was small scale, clandestine. Childish really. But as he moved into the sixth form, and Matty and I to our final year of O-levels, there were more opportunities. For their sixteenth birthdays many kids had parties. Proper parties. The more liberal parents left us to it — which was perfect for Stefan.

Somehow he'd already learned to drive, and at one party (it was nineteen-sixty-five) he managed to get hold of the car keys belonging to the parents of the kid whose party it was. He wanted to go for a drive, he said; wanted to know who was man enough to go with him.

'Manning up'. It was still a journey I was very much on.

Matty didn't want to go, but I bullied him into it. Matty, me, and a kid called Alan, all passengers in a car driven by the testosterone and beer-fuelled Stefan.

As soon as we roared down the street I should have realised we were in trouble. But there was no way out. No chance to stop. Matty begged to be let out, but Stefan wasn't listening. I think Matty's pleas just made him go faster.

On the way out of town there was a railway bridge just before a sharp bend and the canal. As we hurtled towards the arch a car came round the corner. Maybe Stefan was momentarily blinded by its headlights. Or maybe he was never in control at all. The rear of our car clipped the side of the arch. That started the spin. There was no way we were going to make the corner after that.

The car ended up on its side in the water. Alan and I were sitting on the side that remained un-submerged. I don't recall getting out but I did. I do vaguely remember searching for Matty though. And then people arriving to help. Soon after that, the sirens and the blue lights came. Then someone put Alan and me in an ambulance. Just the two of us.

I've hated ambulances ever since.

The rest of that term passed in an odd kind of blur. I wasn't at school much. Teachers sent work home; I did it then sent it back. I only went in for my exams — and ended up passing them all.

Mum and Jack were distraught. They knew it was an accident, just boys being boys, and they said time and again that it wasn't my fault, that they didn't blame me for what happened. What else were they supposed to say? The story they chose to believe was the one printed in the papers: a tragedy; the snuffing out of two young lives filled with potential; the miracle survival of two others.

As if.

~

There was always something about Stefan we didn't trust. Jack especially. Maybe that was a hang-over from the war. He was suspicious of foreigners, even though he denied it. But I knew. Just as I knew I didn't get the whole story; not from you or the police. Stefan's parents tried to paint the whole incident in a totally different light, suggesting you were somehow to blame. How could they not, I suppose? Parents always want to think the best of their children, don't they?

I know I did. Or we did. At least we tried to.

There's no point denying that we wondered 'what if?' from time to time. What if it had been Matty in the front seat? What if he had been the one who'd survived? Or both of you? We still had faith at that stage. "He's just a late bloomer" Jack had said, and seeing what kind of boy you were — almost the inverse of Matty — it was an easy argument to subscribe to. But then, all of a sudden, he wasn't going to bloom at all…

On the one hand that meant we'd never know — and that our dreams for him could never be shattered. On the other hand it also meant all our eggs were suddenly in your basket. Yet even as we recognised that, I could see you slipping away. Jack told me I was being silly, that you were just processing the accident, dealing with it in your own way, growing up. And while that was inevitable of course, I could tell. Even after knowing you for just ten years, I could tell.

Call it a mother's intuition.

~

My own judgement? Not innocent at all.

I'd been the one who'd gone off the rails, who'd not stopped Stefan, who'd forced Matty to get into the car. That was the narrative I created and chose to believe. Who's to say it wasn't true? And surely what I thought was the only thing that counted.

By the end of July I'd finished processing the accident and what it meant. I'd found myself guilty and knew there needed to be some form of punishment. In dreams, I imaged old Whitehurst as the foreman of a jury passing sentence, black cap on his head. His would have been a timely reappearance.

On the assumption that I wouldn't be able to concentrate for a while, that I needed some time 'to heal', the school offered me a year out. But that was the last thing I wanted. Resolved to my fate — and my punishment — I chose to study English, Art and History for A-level. School tried to persuade me against that too. Art and History were far from my strongest subjects, but I wanted to make the next two years as difficult as I could. I told myself I needed to suffer.

And English?

That was a choice prompted by the stories I'd been accumulating; those were what led me there. Something about truth and fiction, the power of lies, the nature of narrative. I'd had first-hand fiction-rich experiences thanks to Martha, Matty, Stefan. Perhaps I wanted to discover how others weaved stories too.

If you wanted me to, I could dress it up better than that, make it a far more profound choice than it actually was. In reality it was no more than a hunch.

And I also knew that studying English wouldn't be easy.

Would Whitehurst have approved of my plan? I knew it didn't matter, wasn't relevant. He might have assumed my redoubled efforts were all about 'not wasting it', but that would have been misinterpretation of the highest order. The road I'd set out on was all about discomfort: three hard subjects, two difficult years, one place at university.

Another new beginning.

Or is that no more than a lazy summary? Juvenile almost. I can do better than that. Surely the sixty-one years between then and now demand I do better, if only to re-recognise that starting anew meant ending something old. "When one door closes…" etcetera. And a door did close. Not close as much as slam shut.

Those A-levels — once again achieving a set of grades no-one bar me was expecting — represented more than the opening of a door, the passport to university and another new stage; they hinted at an opportunity to rid myself of something. Like sloughing a skin. Knowing I was going away — to serious academic pursuits or the serving out of my sentence, you choose — meant I could close another chapter.

On what? Guilt I suppose.

Perhaps I could leave Matty behind. I'd worked hard enough for both of us, got grades good enough for both of us. If there was a bill to be paid then perhaps I decided I'd paid it in the only way I knew how. And if I thought I could leave him behind, maybe I did so without an entirely clean conscience (I think that much is clear!). Perhaps he was merely exorcised to some small degree. Yet in order to become the strong and independent man I wanted to be, I felt I had to shake off *all* the remnants of the life we'd led together.

Oh, you thought I'd been triumphant, that I'd proven myself; you wanted to share in the glory of my success, bask in the reflected glow of being able to tell your friends what I'd achieved, where I was going, my next adventure. There was a future you were only too happy to paint: *my* future as *you* saw it. And with you tangentially linked to it.

Yet I knew my moving on — another new beginning — meant leaving you and Jack. The moment I opened the envelope and stared at the sheet with my grades on it, I saw — not words and letters, nor subjects and single-character assessments (AAB, remember?) — but an image of my hand reaching for a different life. I realised I could walk from one existence to the next and close the door behind me, leaving you in the old room. Abandoned again.

It would be all too easy to pretend that wasn't the case, that our separation — triggered by those three letters 'AAB' — was an incremental one, the inevitable side-effect of a young man growing up. But it wasn't. It was more definitive than that. For me, it was always going to be more than that.

As a result, did you come to feel as if you'd lost your other son too? And if so, when? That day I left on the train laden with my bags? Or when the letters I wrote to you dropped through the letterbox more sporadically? Or that first inter-term holiday I didn't come home? Did you look across the living room one evening towards Jack and say *now I've lost them both*, wordlessly or otherwise?

And what would you say now, if you could?

Chorus

For as long as he could remember he had assumed his life would be dramatic.

How could it not be, born from such violence and violation? And unwillingness too. Not on his part, you understand; he had no say in the matter. Not in the beginning.

And what followed on from his birth? Punishment for a crime he did not commit; a punishment dished out to he and Matthew, proxies for his absconded and anonymous father. Seven years' hard labour. If that wasn't how he saw it early on, perhaps he did so later; perhaps regarding his childhood in such a way came to fit the narrative he chose. Or comes to fit his narrative now. Were that the case, can you blame him if — on occasion — he indulges in a touch of embellishment, attempts to make his early life seem worse than it was? Not that you can possibly know either way. Yet isn't that part of the story-teller's art: weaving and fabricating, blurring the boundaries between fact and fiction? Not that Martha O'Connell was a fabrication. She is a matter of record. Not just his, but the public one too.

The delineation between those two — one person's truth and the public record — has always been a fascination, and for obvious reasons. The car crash wasn't a fiction either; the vehicle ending up in the canal is even less in dispute. Some of his scars were real enough after all.

So what is he doing now? Or trying to do?

If you attempted to tag him with the notion of 'memoir' he would deny it fiercely. *Memoir is for pathetic individuals who have nothing more important to write about than their past selves,* he once said. Maybe so. But he clearly *is* talking about himself.

If not accepting the label of memoir, might he choose to frame his endeavour as no more than 'a narrative' given his penchant for such things? And as you may have already noticed, he has a tendency to close off periods of his life by defining their boundaries — Martha, school, university — and do so in such a way as to use their peripheries to move him on to the next instalment; crossing thresholds, with all that implies. It is very neat and tidy — which in itself may be somewhat incongruous given how his life panned out, a bizarre rollercoaster of literary adventures (if you want to see it that way, that is). But perhaps we should be gracious enough to allow him the luxury of the episodic, especially if he regards that as a suitable way to convey himself from beginning to now… Or to get *us* from A to B. Though this is not a memoir, remember?

More than anything else, he may be trying to sculpt a suitable ending — or indeed to start with one — from which to legitimise his conscious decision to look back; give himself permission to do so. Endings and chapter closings are also about looking forward to the new, starting afresh, the 'hook' to the next. What did he say? *I had to walk from one existence to the next and close the door behind me.* But what if he has suddenly come to realise that there is no 'next'? Under such circumstances what can he do when faced with the compulsion to close a final door? With no 'next', what lies beyond but retreat into the past and the creation of a mausoleum?

If there is a more suitable metaphor for his endeavour, one which is better aligned to his life and those things that have always fascinated him, it may be 'the journey'. Perhaps more specifically, the journey home. Not in the sense of going back to somewhere safe and secure — when did he ever have that! — but rather journey as an attempt to resolve his life, to understand it. Hence his beginning when he wasn't even on the stage.

No. That's not correct. It's too superficial.

What he is trying to do concerns more than comprehension. Memoir and understanding are far too comfortable a pair of bedfellows to apply to him. He might argue that one of the main reasons people write memoir is to comprehend their life, to make it tangible, to set in stone both the nature of it and its progression. And to prove they existed long after they are no longer around to offer that evidence in person. Yet although he may be doing just that — tackling memoir — the act of writing it may be no more than by-product of something more important. Retrospective journeying from A to B is of little interest to him unless it does more than build a temporal map. His obsession (if you haven't picked up on it already) is proof of self: challenge, justification and judgement — Martha, Whitehurst, examinations. And with more to come. His is a journey replayed from the paradoxical insecurity of the courtroom dock. Expounded and partially interpreted, he is offering up his life and work to be valued and weighed. To be judged.

Which, of course, makes you the jury.

~

Without doubt, there is tension in his testimony (and in the testimony of others); not in terms of veracity — though as a juror you should always be concerned with that! — but in how such testimonies are articulated. You might decide he is obsessed with fiction and in consequence conclude that the evidence he presents may be little more than an amalgam of stories. If so, then your role is to separate fact from fabrication, the truth from the lies. He has already told you how, from an early age, he was exposed to the power of lies. Collectively these might have proven a more effective tutor than Whitehurst could ever have hoped to be.

But the tension — or the irony, if you prefer — may not bubble-up from the narrative's surface, but via the only tools he has available to him to craft his story. Narrative and fiction (call it what you will) is delivered through words, through language; and language therefore carries the burden not only of the storytelling but of the journey itself. Or is writing a journey in its own right, a mechanism for unravelling the past and dousing it in the gloss of the contemporaneous? History varnished? More than that; might it not also be the conduit for judgement, whether yours or his own: 'guilty' or 'not guilty'?

Is this medium to be trusted therefore, his words serving at least two masters? Walking the tightrope between fact and fiction, past and present, truth and lies, plea and judgement — language can be slippery and untrustworthy. Indeed, it *must* be so. All of which makes *your* job so much harder.

It would be entirely understandable if, as a result, you felt at a disadvantage — after all, you are essentially playing the game on his terms, being led like a bull with a ring through its nose or a horse by its bridle; led into the show-ring where judgement is passed or value assigned. Seeing beyond such shepherding — or through it — will be the trick.

So some clues then, to see if they help…

- At university his favourite book — to both read and study — was *Ulysses*. He was fascinated by Joyce's manipulation of language, how it became a fluid thing in his hands, how stylistically the novel was so divergent, how it purported to be one thing yet was simultaneously something else, both honest and untrustworthy.

- At one time or another, he also had a fascination for mythology, especially classical Greek and Roman: Zeus and his clan; Mount Olympus and man's relationship with the gods; the Trojan War. Obviously this would have provided additional depth to his relationship with *Ulysses*, especially in terms of Joyce using Odysseus' journey home as a template for the structure of his book.

- If he feels a kinship with Stephen Daedalus and Leopold Bloom (and even Molly, who knows!) then it arises from the collisions between Joyce's work and the legends which lay behind it. Perhaps this kinship stretches a little further in that Charles may regard his own life as somehow mythological. If so, is he Odysseus or Leopold, Molly or Stephen? Or some mash-up of them? Does he see himself as fundamentally 'heroic'?

- Given all that, to what extent is his 'memoir' (which is not a memoir remember!) a journey akin to those of the *fictional* or *mythological* characters which fascinate him? Will that be how he frames his narrative? Or is he — like Odysseus — simply trying to find a way 'home'? And if so, when we are judging him — when *you* are judging him — are you also passing sentence on the notion of mythology, on *Ulysses*, on Joyce and *his* characters? On all of that — even on the concept of 'home'...? That might be a stretch, but it is one some people could try and make.

- And finally (if this isn't too much of a leap) might we not consider all the characters in his 'non-memoir' — his mother, Martha, Jack, Whitehurst, Stefan, Matty — as figures from mythology too? *His* mythology. If so, what does that imply in relation to your judgement, not only on him but on any of it?

And what of me, you may ask?

Perhaps think of me as the opening Chorus — in the Greek sense, obviously! And how fitting to do so. A disinterested guide to get you started, to set the scene — though I'll soon leave the rest of the book to him; it's his journey after all...

~

But to return to the concrete — and to another parallel. Like Odysseus, our narrator's existence is framed by the sea.

Charles was born — conceived and born — in Brighton, on the south coast of England in 1949. It was a place beginning its own kind of journey even then: a slide (as some might regard it) away from the genteel to the raucous, the garish, the loud and down-market. Given the nature of the place, his mother wouldn't have been the only young woman to find herself abused, taken advantage of, made victim.

The O'Connells — who took he and Matty nowhere at all in terms of adventures or holidays — were ensconced in Portsmouth, a little further west along the coast. The naval port had its own slice of low-life, the brash; yet in places it was also genteel, even refined. It was in such areas of the city Martha and Timothy aspired to live, holed-up as they were in a small terraced house in Fratton not far from the football ground. Occasionally they would get as far as the seafront; once or twice they took the train to Southampton. If they ever talked about 'going home' and returning to Ireland, it would have been a conversation without any real intent behind it.

Towards the end, when the shackles were occasionally loosened, the twins would take themselves off to the beach for an afternoon. In those days it was acceptable for children to do that — especially if they were not cared about. Yet up to that last early-summer in Portsmouth neither of them were conscious of the Brighton connection. They didn't become aware of their geographic origins until, aged seven, they moved to live with Valerie and Jack in Chichester, a third of the way between Portsmouth and Brighton.

It is not known whether — via a combination of Jack's stories and Portsmouth's naval history — Charles ever made a connection between the Second World War and the Trojan War, or between the D-Day landings and the Trojan Horse itself. It would not have been impossible for him to have done so. His step-father's North African mythology may have been set on a different continent, but it was one geographically closer to the scene of the Greeks' triumph over the Trojans than the south coast of England.

He gave up the sea when he gave up his mother. It was another instance of divorce and physical separation. Offered a place at Southampton University, studying there proved a tempting proposition for a while, but he talked himself out of it: too close, too easy. If he still needed to punish himself for Matty's death, that punishment had to include both removal from the familiar *and* the insertion of distance. Sheffield was a long way from the south coast; indeed, it was a fair march from any coast. There he would be out of his comfort zone, geographically, intellectually, emotionally. Unsettling that triumvirate was a task he regarded as essential for the next segment of his life.

Sailing from one safe harbour with the intent of eventually finding another, perhaps.

The journey. The quest.

Or an escape. That's an interesting notion, especially in his case.

He has painted the picture of leaving Chichester as compulsion, the need to move on "from one existence to the next" — and as the price he had to pay for Matty's death. So a running toward something too? You could argue that. Redemption? Forgiveness? Or was it not more likely to have been an attempt to flee the past — his mother's, Martha, Matty? The chanting of others (who, just like Martha, doubted he would ever amount to much) were voices he would never exorcise.

And he would come across others expressing similar negative opinions soon enough; their timbres may have been different, but not the message. And the loudest of these? Perhaps that voice in his head which — although variously disguised — nagged at him, doubted his talent, claimed he was an imposter.

But isn't that the nature of journeys, both leaving something behind and needing to arrive elsewhere? Odysseus leaving Troy, wanting to get home; Bloom leaving his house to go breakfast-shopping before his day-long journey and the return to the unfaithful Molly; Daedalus, leaving the Martello tower and heading — somewhere… Is he all three of those?

It might have appealed to him to consider his life in such terms, his 'episodes' fragments of a greater whole.

Don't be surprised if that is how he frames his narrative, one way or another…

But now the court is in session. Listen up. My job here is done.

Lion

1967 - 1969

Odd how beginnings are harder to recall than endings.

Or is it? I suppose we're instinctively drawn to the climax of things because that's where the conclusive action is, where issues get resolved. There's rawness in attachment, either way.

I can't really remember those first few days in Sheffield. They must have been exciting after a fashion — new town, new place to live, meeting new people — but other than that? There were events for virgin students to 'ease us in'. Not many, but some. These seemed to be focussed on drinking, as if that was the first module of every academic course: discovery of alcohol, finding your limits, working out what booze did to you.

Given events in my recent past, I abstained. Having already been exposed to its potentially calamitous and life-changing (life-ending!) consequences, I told myself I would never drink again. Inevitably it was a resolution destined to last just a short while — but at least long enough to avoid the all-too-common outcomes of those pre-course days: getting drunk and throwing up; or booze-fuelled collisions which sometimes resulted in unexpected or ill-advised sex. In a few instances these rapidly grew into a commitment for life — the ultimate negative lesson perhaps and, for some, becoming a situation from which it proved impossible to reverse...

But I told myself that wasn't why I was there, to enjoy myself, to indulge in experimental dalliances. Doing so wouldn't have satisfied my 'suffering' agenda; wouldn't have aligned with my higher purpose.

If that's how I saw it, of course.

And if I did, what a pompous git!

When my course started the formal work was sufficiently challenging for me to throw myself into it wholeheartedly and allow the routine to envelop me. It was perfect being told what to read, where to be at what time, what the assignments were, and when essays needed to be handed in. In case this retrospective response comes across as abdication, I never regarded it in that way, but rather — and obscurely — as a kind of freedom; my timetable freed me *not* to think about what to do. Academically, at least. It allowed me the space to search for a place (in the widest possible sense) in which I would be happy to 'live'.

One of the few extra-curricular things I tried, the Creative Writing Group (somewhat misnamed in the dim and distant past as 'The Hive') was an English department staple. It had been running for years. Every September it was disturbed by an influx of over-zealous first-year students, the majority of whom would have drifted away by the end of October, the absconders most likely to have fallen prey to the ongoing lure of drink or sex. Or both. Some people discovered they were natural 'party animals'…

In my first Hive meeting there were two third-years (the hardened veterans), five second-years, and about ten of us newbies. Something like that, though the precise numbers hardly matter. It was a standard distribution for lots of the university's clubs and societies: the closer people came to finals, the more their priorities changed. By mid-October the numbers were already down to one, three, and five.

Which was perfect for me.

I can't really remember the format, not precisely. There were exercises, themes; occasionally one or two members of staff might drop in, usually in relation to some challenge or other. For example, one week we agreed to write some stream of consciousness fiction akin to the closing section of *Ulysses*, and Frank dropped in to set the scene for us. In this way The Hive's process was similar to course homework or being set an essay: challenge given, a week to respond, then read the offering at the following meeting. It also provided a timetable, a framework all its own.

Again, perfect.

Was anything we wrote any good? Probably not. At least not at first. Inevitably we looked up to those who had survived The Hive the longest and mentally gifted them a talent based on that longevity — talent they may or may not have had. Most often not. We newbies were aspirational, though we didn't want to be like our more experienced peers but rather Yeats or Auden, Amis or Conrad. And yes, even Joyce. Traditional, experimental; we trotted out pages of rudimentary pastiche. Me included.

And?

We thought it all wonderful of course, but most of what we wrote was nonsense. Blunt, unimaginative stuff. I was inexperienced enough to think I had to club words into submission in order to get them to say what I wanted them to. Though half the time I didn't, of course. Know what I wanted to say, I mean — and even when I did, I didn't manage to get the words to say it.

But it also became about something more specific. I discovered the particular beast I wanted to slay was the one which guarded the *telling* of stories: not so much the words in the stories, but how you mapped out and then unfolded your narrative, laid it out for the reader. And not just the structure, but the rhythm, the pace. It was weaving really.

And though I know structure, rhythm and pace is all in the words — where else could it be! — in those early days I thought I could divorce the two. More nonsense of course.

There were those in The Hive who aspired to other things, other goals. Most of the males wanted to be poets. They had images of themselves as 'Romantics' and were trying to craft some kind of contemporary Byronesque vibe — both in their work and, in one or two cases, how they lived their lives. Poets *and* party animals, you might say. Others were dabbling in all sorts, trying things on for size, like being effete or gay or sullen. Soon enough I realised the majority lacked both the talent and commitment to see anything through.

Don't get me wrong. Back then I didn't know I had talent. Suspicions, yes; but certainty? I doubt it. I was committed, both to the course and The Hive; never missed a lecture or a session. Mine was a kind of feeding frenzy, two halves of my life symbiotic, knowledge and experience in one helping the other.

More weaving maybe.

I know some thought I was too keen, too earnest, too intense; that I took it, well, too seriously. But I'd found something I didn't want to let go of — even if, in those early days, I couldn't articulate exactly what that precious thing was nor why I had become so addicted to it.

And it *was* an addiction. Look up any dictionary definition of addiction and substitute 'me' and 'writing' somewhere within it and you'll get a sense of what it became. And quickly too. Each week, each theme, each challenge; all were drug-like 'hits' which added to my stock of experience, my portfolio of work. Faulty work of course, especially early on; but learnings, always. During that first year my formal grades gradually improved — not because my academic knowledge was growing any more profound, but because I was getting better at how I articulated what little I knew, elucidated theories, teased out propositions. Told the story.

I remember at the end of one essay Frank wrote *a pleasure to read*. My first real triumph.

It was I suppose (and to use a modern trope) like finding you had a superpower. A bit like Peter Parker, I had been bitten by some kind of bug and was just beginning to realise the consequences. Not merely that. Each week I learned a little more in terms of how to wield that power, whether it was in an essay on Dickens or a flash fiction challenge in the writing group.

By the middle of the second term something had changed: my status in The Hive. I found I was being listened to more, asked to read first, to suggest topics for the following week. Perhaps having people wanting to see what I had written was the most powerful drug of all.

If I found a niche, a style people liked, I would run with it for two or three weeks, experimenting with the narratives or themes that style might be able to carry. I elaborated or pared back, told outrageous lies or equally outrageous truths. It was the flexing of muscle. When people could no longer trust the veracity of my words and didn't know what to believe, when they were enthralled and bound by what I'd written, then I knew I had something.

Okay, that's how I choose to frame it now, to think of it as a superpower; but back then? I was probably too drunk on my embryonic status and its attendant ounce of recognition to think of it as 'a power' at all.

Yet if you think back to my original ambitions for university, this second routine was hardly punishment at all; wouldn't you agree? Not considering how things turned out. And so quickly too.

You might ask whether I abandoned the notion of college as the undertaking of something difficult, as serving my sentence (the irony in the multiple meanings of that word!); and, if so, when that abandonment occurred. At what point did my conviction (in the legal sense) become irrelevant, trumped by the newer conviction to pursue my writing? Another duality. If it did — and it must have done! — I can't tell you *exactly* when that was. It might have been after the first few days or after the first few months... I hadn't forgotten Matty (how could I?) but I think by Easter any sense of debt or the paying of dues was fading fast. My experience — especially in The Hive — had morphed into something else; it had become all about me and what I was discovering.

And who I was striving to become.

Was that too self-centred? Too egotistical? I can't possibly say. However, what I *do* know is that by the end of my first year I was established: one of the guiding lights in The Hive and a solid academic performer who might just get a First if I pulled my finger out. Whitehurst all over again! Of course I didn't 'pull my finger out' and I didn't get a First either…

Although I wasn't The Hive 'top dog' come the end of June, I was heading that way; and as the new academic year dawned — and as I took my turn to become one of those ready to welcome in September's new intake of aspirational wannabes — a certain 'unofficial' role began to attach itself to me. I still don't believe it was something I sought, though that may just be hindsight talking. Or a desire to try and present myself with a degree of modesty.

~

I went home but briefly that first summer. A couple of weeks at most. Between leaving halls late and returning early, the rest of the vacation was spent visiting friends in their homes, sofa-surfing in London, Manchester, Bristol. Even an uncomfortable camping trip to mid-Scotland with a fleeting girlfriend. Uncomfortable in every sense! The one constant across that whole period, June to September, was my working on a script for a short play. Hardly original, the idea was stolen from a true story about a Japanese soldier who was hiding in an Asian jungle unaware that the Second World War was over. My version was set in England; a two-handed piece about a Norfolk farmer who'd captured a German pilot whose plane had been shot down and who had parachuted onto his land. *Tainted Harvest* was the rather pretentious title.

The farmer, armed with his shotgun, had locked the airman in one of his farm's outbuildings. It was, I suppose, a story about punishment and lack of freedom. The farmer — whose son had died in the siege of Calais — wanted revenge, and the pilot's sudden arrival provided him with a means to execute that revenge. He knows he should immediately give the airman up to the authorities, but as that awareness strengthens he finds the idea of surrendering him harder and harder to contemplate.

From what I recall it was all very wordy, the stage split in two with 'a wall' down the centre (very Pyramus and Thisbe!): farmer on one side, German on the other. In their individual ways they are both guilty, torn. Over the course of the play they come to understand each other a little, and an embryonic respect grows.

~

FARMER   Did you think you were going to die?

AIRMAN   When?

FARMER   When you were shot down.

AIRMAN   What do you think?

The FARMER shifts his weight from one foot to the other; takes a step forward; reaffirms the grip on his gun.

FARMER   Tell me.

AIRMAN   Of course I did. [*pause*] But it was over in a moment. There was the shock of a shell bursting nearby, the sudden lurch of the plane, my loss of control. I felt the plane starting to spin. I was scared in that moment.

FARMER   What did you think would happen then?

AIRMAN   That the plane would explode. Or I wouldn't get out. Perhaps for a second... [*pause*] And then instinct took over. I unbuckled; got the cockpit open; somehow threw myself out.

FARMER   You thought you were safe?

AIRMAN   As soon as my parachute opened — and when I
             saw there were none of your planes nearby.

FARMER   We wouldn't shoot a man coming down in a
             parachute. [*with some heat*] We're not animals.

*The FARMER eases himself back against the wall; regathers
himself. Although his pose looks relaxed, there is an air of
resignation in it. The AIRMAN shifts on the hay-bale on which
he sits.*

FARMER   So you thought you were going to die for, what, a
             few seconds at most? [*pause; looks down*] My
             son must have thought he was going to die every
             second of every day he was trapped in Calais:
             your bombs and shells, the constant barrage. Not
             just for a few moments. [*pause; looks back at the
             AIRMAN*] Can you imagine what that must have
             been like, to be trapped in fear for so long?
             Perhaps he longed for the blast that would put
             him out of his misery. Perhaps he welcomed
             oblivion when it came.

*The FARMER lowers his head again. From the other side of the
stall where he is bound, the AIRMAN watches him, shifts
again; looks down at the parachute cords which have betrayed
him and become his restraints.*

AIRMAN   [*slowly*] I too am a father.

*The FARMER straightens, moves away from the wall, waves
his gun toward the stall.*

FARMER   [*with venom*] You don't count. You and your
             kind, you're nothing.

The FARMER leaves the barn.

~

Okay, let's be honest; it was all pretty derivative. Beckett with
bits of Brecht thrown in. The uni drama group were keen to
put it on that December. I'd slept with one of the committee
members two or three times so she helped my cause. In the
end they ran it as a one-off show in the last week of term. The

small auditorium we used was about three-quarters full. It was a great success. People loved it.

And then, as a result, everything changed.

Tainted Harvest was suddenly my first real triumph; something I could wear around my neck as if it was a medal. I was now 'a playwright' — even if I wasn't. There was an attendant degree of respect which manifested itself at the first meeting of The Hive in January. From that moment I knew it was *my* group and in consequence assumed I'd be able to mould it to do my bidding for the next eighteen months. *My* group. *My* Hive. I was the one — the only one — who'd actually proven themselves.

Oh, looking back it's impossible not to acknowledge I was merely playing at being a writer — we all were — but in that heady cocooned environment? I thought I'd made it, even if I hadn't. Big fish in a small pond perhaps — though in truth, not even that. I didn't realise just how minuscule the pond was, nor the true nature of my 'status'. But that didn't matter. It wasn't exactly the beginning of a new phase in the same way that going to college had been (or leaving Martha's, come to that), but it was a significant moment, an adjustment in trajectory.

If I'm honest, from that point on I looked at those Byronesque-types with fresh eyes; I'd gained an insight into why they were as they were and what they were trying to attain. It was the lure of 'the artistic life' — whatever that might mean — and for a short period I was almost tempted. Not Byron (never Byron!) but someone else perhaps. There were enough idols on whom to model oneself: John Osborne, the young Dennis Potter, Beckett. Even Joyce.

The result? I drank a little more; took up smoking for effect; enhanced my reputation — warranted or otherwise — for playing 'fast and loose' with members of the fairer sex…

Given all that's now long in the past, usurped by other moments, ambitions and so forth, it's easy to regard that new life as being a bit of a game, the trying out of a fresh personality — because I don't think I ever went 'all in', even if it had been very real and very immediate at the time. I couldn't. I knew that underlying everything — the drinking, the smoking, the sex — was something important but embryonic: a scratty little play about a PoW, and what I'd achieved with a few hundred words. Compared to that everything else was just insubstantial fluff. I also began to think that academic status — however modest — was merely surface-dressing versus the future my creative words might offer me. Like safety, security. Although unaware of it, brick by brick I'd been building a defensive wall since before I was seven-years-old. Or word by word. *Tainted Harvest* was akin to setting the last stone, or providing the mechanism for a drawbridge I could finally pull up.

I found I had been rewarded with the ability to absent myself from the mundane on my own terms. Not retreat in the sense of running away or becoming a hermit, but rather to remove a part of myself to a place where I was more secure. And yet simultaneously I was being more outgoing, trying to live a new kind of life. Which sounds contradictory, doesn't it? But I don't think so. It was the beginning of two different versions of me; words' superpower offered me the chance to recognise the two, and understand what they were. Or what they could potentially become.

'Public' and 'private'? Possibly. Probably.

Over that same period, those first eighteen months in Sheffield, they manifested themselves as weapons too. Words, that is. Isn't that what weapons do, allow you to both attack and defend? I'd previously learned how cruel they could be and that they could inflict pain. Martha, of course. But as a child, how could I possibly have understood that? How could anyone? Not at first. Matty and I were simply on the receiving end, barb after barb, blow after blow. Both verbal and physical. And now here I was, tables turned.

Not that I abused people with my new power you understand. Not knowingly. Or at least not painfully. Nor intentionally. I had others for that. My characters. The farmer and the German, for example. I could put those through the wringer, have them suffer 'the slings and arrows'. It was a capability of which I wasn't fully conscious when the play was staged, but as I grew into the new year…

Well, you learn, don't you?

The most satisfying aspect of this burgeoning was discovering the ability to create new realities, and then — having created them — to twist and alter and undermine. Not just for the fictional characters of course, but for the audience too. Saying one thing and meaning another; wrapping up a lie in a big pink bow and presenting it as truth, a gift. Knotting and unravelling, unravelling and knotting.

Were you to push me (and push me hard) I might confess that this — what shall we call it? — 'manipulation', occasionally bled into the 'real world'. If others managed to scale my castle walls or skip over the drawbridge and into an unplanned skirmish, then I'd have to confess that some consequent incidents (few and far between, you understand!) might have been unpleasant, not for my fictional characters but for me. And for those others too. In their own way they were doing something similar. Other people, I mean. We were all creating stories. It was a hormone-fuelled time; everyone was learning, experimenting, finding themselves. There were emotional corpses all over the place — but at least I had my security, the safety-net of being able to expose and examine myself on the page via a whole raft of proxies. The privilege and protection of anonymous public dissection.

See what I mean?

And now?

Well, old habits die hard.

Or they never die at all. It's groove which, having found, I've been occupying ever since. Wearing it out, or down; whatever you do with grooves. Deepen them, I suppose. When does a groove become a rut?

Very philosophical!

But don't make the mistake of thinking I was falling into a trap, or that my metaphorical castle became something which constrained or confined me. The complete opposite is true. Honestly. I was freed. Totally. Entirely. My recently embraced superpower — an ability to play with stories — was wholly liberating. Having never been truly free before, I was released from the chains of Martha and Portsmouth, Valerie and Jack in Chichester. Even Valerie's Brighton history. And Matty?

The cornerstone of that freedom was discovery. Self-discovery: who I was; what I was capable of doing. More than that, my first triumph allowed me to sweep away the mythic bonds of an expected or prescribed future: that I would do this, do that, go here, go there. If I'd never had any aspiration other than to pay my debt to Matty, I now found I could look up, look forward. Was I unshackled? Did I consider my debt repaid?

Don't misunderstand me. Don't assume that by my second Easter in Sheffield I'd mapped out some grand plan for my future. Perhaps the most significant thing of all was nothing more than the satisfaction of knowing I *had* a future; one which, although nebulous, could be positively anticipated. One which (as I saw it at the time) didn't rely on chance.

But even that's a little disingenuous. I was still naïve, of course I was. Perhaps I thought the future would be one glorious victory after another. How could it not be, right? I'd already started work on a new project and, having just escaped the bonds of being 'a teenager', how could I *not* (in my innocence) have made the assumption that whatever followed *Tainted Harvest* would be a masterpiece? That's the problem with superpowers; they make you think you're invincible — until someone arrives bearing kryptonite.

In any event, there I was 'setting sail'. The future looked glorious and I would be immortal.

And now, glancing in the rear-view mirror?

Well, as recently attested to medically, I can confirm that I'm *not* immortal. Nor can I boast of a life-long unbroken string of triumphs. That's one of the interesting things about looking back, this re-examining of events through an entirely different lens. How can my perspective, fifty-seven years further down the road, be anything but altered? Naïvety versus wisdom, innocence versus experience. And all built upon those bedrock years of battles and fights, victories and defeats. It — this 'non-memoir' — is not merely a retrospective re-living, but a back-tracking too. An unravelling. Interesting notion, 'back-tracking'. It implies both going back over old ground *and* the undoing of those things; perhaps replacing one truth with another, or one lie with another. Or truths with lies. And so forth.

As if I would…

And it's a journey too. If the farmer and the German effectively unlocked my future and gave me the opportunity to get my head up and look forward, then such activity was only scratching the surface in terms of foreseeing what might lay ahead; imaging the 'quest', if you like. And perhaps this writing, these words, this 'work', is another quest. Or an alternative incarnation of the same one. Especially if a 'quest' is all about finding something, seeking resolution. Or judgement.

But that's enough sugar-coating.

Hydra

1970

The other day I 'Googled' myself. Spent an hour or so scraping the barrel-bottom of the internet to see what I could find, the composite picture of me painted there. A little like an Identikit image I suppose, or those silly card games kids used to have back in the day where you could mix-and-match attributes of faces, upper-body clothes, lower-body clothes. It now seems odd that we should have invented games to encourage children to laugh at people. *Look at his belly! Look at her nose!*

My internet scavaging was a delving I'd prefer to regard more as research than vanity.

Anyway, having followed a few blind alleys and seen too many duplications of the same data, the same reviews, the same lists and opinions, I came across a reference to The Hive. I hadn't been looking for it, nor expected to see one, but there it was; two left turns, then three right, down two flights of stairs, last door on the left. Internet-wise. It was tagged with the university, its alumni, my name; the algorithm putting fragments together as if it was trying to find the best image to align with a jumble of jigsaw pieces.

The site was purporting to show those students who had, at one time or another, been members of The Hive. The list started about ten years before my sojourn in Sheffield, and ended about ten years after. Did that coincide with the demise of the group or was it simply an arbitrary end-point? I couldn't tell. Somehow I suspected the former. Most of the names I didn't recognise, but a small proportion I did. Obviously.

Imogen Brearley's leapt from the screen and slapped me round the face.

How long had it been since I'd thought of her?

Believe it or not, Imogen was one of the few people to whom I've ever taken an instant dislike. Physically there was nothing remarkable about her — in the same way, I suppose, that there's nothing remarkable about most of us; we're all more or less 'average'. But rather than being middling or mediocre, I came to think of Imogen as a 'nearly' person: she was nearly very pretty; nearly very intelligent; nearly a very good writer. Distracted from my internet self-search, I followed her own breadcrumb trail for a few clicks to discover she'd gone into journalism for a while — which would have suited her — and then from mainstream newspapers into magazines; perhaps a shift which would have suited her less. Then she seemed to disappear from view. Presumably married, children, no longer working. For some reason I felt a pang — and not because of any regret that we'd never made a connection. Romantically, I mean. As I said, I'd not really liked her.

She was in my cohort, my intake year; yet academically our paths rarely crossed. Her passion was sixteenth century poetry, Chaucer, Old English; she was openly hostile to Modernism, Post-structuralism and the like. She thought Freud was a con-artist and people like Chomsky, Lacan, and Foucault clowns.

Though none of that was really the issue.

As far as The Hive was concerned, Imogen joined it at the beginning of the spring term in our first year. She was immediately combative. She loved form and structure, poetry that rhymed; she was a traditionalist, non-experimental, and she wasn't afraid to make that plain. She distrusted prose — which proved to be somewhat ironic given her eventual profession. Her modus operandi seemed to be to criticise anything she didn't understand rather than make the effort to try and do so. Or at least that was my assessment.

On that basis, at least once every meeting we'd find ourselves on the opposite sides of an argument. From time to time it felt as if she was trying to convert me, to get me to see the error of my ways and turn me back towards the light. And I suppose I did likewise.

Publicly neither of us were prepared to give an inch; the harder one pushed, the more the other dug their heels in. Our little exchanges must have been fascinating for others to observe, especially those who were less 'resolved'. Most of them probably couldn't have cared less. I confess I occasionally tried some of the things she suggested — a sonnet here, a sestina there — but these were experiments carried out in secret, their output never made public. I didn't want to give her that satisfaction. Whether she did likewise I can't say, though I'd like to think I had some positive influence on her. Perhaps if that had happened — i.e. we'd both confessed to the odd piece of stylistically atypical scribbling — we might have become friends. It wouldn't have been inconceivable.

But we didn't.

Twelve months later, after the success of my play — and my grip on the group tightening as a result — she stopped coming. At the time it was probably a relief; after all, Imogen had been the person most willing to 'rock the boat'. Her withdrawal made my life easier.

And yet…

Looking back can do funny things to memory can't it? On reflection, I think I actually missed her attendance at The Hive — not that there was any way I could have seen it at the time. More than that, I'm now free to acknowledge what she did for me during those twelve months or so when we collided: the challenging, the pushing, not letting me have it too easy. Yes, and even the sonnets and sestinas! One way or another I think Imogen made me a better writer. Oh, her influence would have been marginal, her overall contribution minuscule, but it would be wrong of me not to come clean, to reflect upon that.

Maybe it's too late. Maybe when she reads this she'll smile, reminisce, think about me more more kindly. Though having said that, and considering our shared past, I suspect she's hardly likely to have ever read any of my stuff. At least not benevolently.

~

He wasn't arrogant. Not in the beginning. We were all in the same boat, aspiring to something for which we had no label, no name. Floundering enthusiastically. That's how I thought of us for a while; all of us.

In a way it was like being thrown from a ship into a rough sea and seeing who would survive. In a way. Under those circumstances having something to cling to was important; vital in my case. So I held fast to what I knew and loved, what I believed wouldn't let me down. Most others had nothing like that; you could tell those who were going to drown. The first week they didn't turn up to The Hive you were never surprised.

There were a very few who didn't seem to need life vests, or a raft, or some fragment to cling to; yet I never saw Charles as one of those. Not really. When he got his break and they put his play on, well, that was like some celestial hand throwing him a lifebuoy or teaching him to swim — though I'm not sure that's how he saw it. Whatever; it meant he was able to keep his head above the water more easily than the rest of us.

I'm sure he thought he'd been gifted some fancy motorboat!

I suppose there was a modicum of reflected benefit for the rest of us, a coincidental inheritance — if only an awareness of what might be possible, and that we could be saved. Or could save ourselves.

Even though I tried to keep going to The Hive (and tried hard), I don't have any problem confessing that I gave up. In the face of the onslaught (and you can read that any way you choose!), one day I simply bailed. It wasn't that I couldn't write — something proven by my subsequent career of course — but rather that I couldn't write under those circumstances, in a regime that was beginning to be shaped according to some set of unwritten rules. His rules. My own buoyancy aids started to fail me, to disintegrate — and I didn't want to drown.

Or to be drowned.

Sometimes the wake Charles created was more destructive than the sea itself.

~

I don't think it unreasonable to regard her as 'my first real critic' — if you take a critic to be someone who challenges you, pushes hard against what you've produced, or questions it and takes some convincing of its merit. But then, based on that definition, what's an 'unreal' critic? Those who claim what you've produced is rubbish and make no attempt to say why they think so nor offer anything constructive? With the unreal critic you can't possibly win; there is no argument to which they will listen, partly because they're certain they're right — or don't care if they are wrong — and because they know that entering into a debate is likely to expose *them* more than it will you, so they simply don't do so. After all these years I've had my fair share of both types. The critic is a many-headed beast.

Even if Imogen's starting point was that whatever I wrote was likely to compromise the boundaries of what she thought of as 'good writing', I now choose to believe she didn't regard me as totally unredeemable — why else would she have made her suggestions about form or challenge me to try other things? She wouldn't have wasted her time if she felt I was a hopeless case. I have to give her credit for that. And I'm also prepared to credit that she was a fully paid-up member of the kind of critiquing clan who will eventually give ground when they recognise you've produced something worthwhile — it's just that they take an awful lot of persuading!

So there's a boundary separating the two sorts of critic, 'real' and 'unreal'; an invisible line of indeterminate thickness. A line which — perhaps in spite of herself — Imogen may have occasionally crossed.

In 1970 I was twenty-one. At forty-six, Rufus Horberry was more than twice my age. When the university put on a play or suchlike, it was never quite a closed event. Made aware of the show, connected outsiders would occasionally pitch up, sit somewhere at the back. Often they would leave early.

Scanning the audience throughout the performance of *Tainted Harvest* that second December (checking faces for reactions, of course!) if I had noticed him at all I would probably have assumed he was some visiting academic. The few times I subsequently saw him he was always immaculately dressed — 'dapper' is the best word to describe him — and as such would have fit the mould of 'the sub-standard academic': all show and no substance. By then though I'd discovered he was a hack who worked for the local rag, their 'Arts and Culture' columnist.

I didn't see his review until January when it was pointed out to me by Imogen, as if in doing so she was delivering conclusive proof of my ineptitude — and that she had been right all along. Attempting to hammer the first nail into my literary coffin perhaps.

Horberry had gone to town. He'd hated my play with a vengeance, and — ignoring the reaction of just about everyone else who had been in the auditorium — ran through a gamut of lazy put-downs with apparently unrestrained glee. 'Derivative' seemed to be his favourite word, closely followed by 'unimaginative', 'clichéd', 'shallow', 'trite'... I could go on.

None of this resonated with me, of course. They were the ravings of a critic of dubious vintage delivered from behind the security of a typewriter and desk protected by thick office walls; akin to an internet troll in contemporary parlance. Given the choice between his view and the more general and generous approbation — including from some of the course lecturers — I was always going to want to relegate his opinion to the waste-bin.

Except I found I couldn't.

Whether we like it or not, every time someone says something about our work it raises a question. Most often it's superficial — "is it really that good / bad?" — yet even so, *any* question is problematic for a writer. No matter who asks it, the asking is like laying a mine in the acreage between you and your next work. The only way to clear those mines is to produce that next play or story or whatever, and then move on — even if the new work eventually, and inevitably, leads to the next minefield.

Horberry was an expert in the laying of mines. It was his bread-and-butter; what he enjoyed doing. And — if I'm honest — what he was brutally good at. I can imagine him after he submitted another piece of copy, sitting back, congratulating himself on blowing someone else to smithereens. As a target for his sabotage — and a novice to boot — I had limited choices: I could ignore the explosive devices and walk confidently across the landscape certain I would not be blown-up, or I could tread gingerly, acknowledging and then choosing to disarm or navigate my way around each one. Where Imogen was concerned, my tactic had varied; I either ignored her traps or diffused the ones I knew I could.

I showed Frank the review. He was very much in the 'walk right on through' camp: *If Rufus was any good, he'd be the one writing original material rather than sniping from the sidelines.* Turned out Frank knew him of old.

But I was twenty-one. For all my bluster and bravado, I was still green. Horberry knew that. It made me an even more legitimate target. Easy meat.

Though it was the only significant review he would ever write about my work — and even though I would, to all intents and purposes, 'move on' — I found I wasn't able to ignore the mines. 'Derivative', 'clichéd'. They were just waiting to be stepped on. So I did. I re-examined *Tainted Harvest* time and again searching for flaws. For a while I played with the text, making changes. I was trying to put myself in Horberry's shoes, trying to see what he had seen, and then, having found the flaws, put them right. It was a pointless task. After a while the play seemed to become something else: something I hadn't written; something that failed to hang together; something that was suddenly worse than it had been. The text-mines going off I suppose.

And as if that negative outcome wasn't bad enough, I found myself adopting Horberry's position when it came to new things I was writing. The microscope under which I examined them was turned up to maximum focus; my starting position shifted from "this is probably good" to "this must be bad". More often than I would have wanted I found myself re-working drafts over and over, and in that reworking drove myself further and further from what I'd intended to say.

I'd started to lay my own mines. The Hydra's heads were multiplying.

Given Imogen had just about left the group by this point, I didn't even have her marginally more constructive criticism to fall back on. That may have been when I unwittingly started to miss her. If I ever did.

Not that I let my insecurity show. I couldn't afford to do that given the elevated status which had been bestowed on me and my work. Or which I'd purloined, I suppose. 'Emperor's New Clothes'? It crossed my mind. For the remainder of that second academic year I allowed myself to focus more on the group, the schedule of what we did, the structure of things. I read less of my own work but strived to contribute more. Perhaps there was a desire to be positive, constructive, helpful — something born from not wishing to end up like Horberry. If it was self-defence, just about everyone in the group misread it; they thought I was stepping-up, sharing the benefit of my wisdom, my talent. But in a sense I was running away. To an extent, Horberry had popped the balloon of my success. He would have been delighted to discover that I'd convinced myself I wasn't good enough.

At least temporarily.

I could be magnanimous with Horberry in the way I think I've been with Imogen, recognise what he did for me in terms of getting me to question my work more strenuously, strive to make it better. But I'm not going to. It all comes down to intent. Agree with her or not, approve of her approach or otherwise, on reflection I think Imogen's interventions were nearly always rooted in honourable principles. Horberry's never were. He was like a locust: all he wanted to do was destroy and move on.

How close did he come?

Close enough. In a way, that second academic year's final term saved me. That and The Hive.

~

"Charles E's debut, Tainted Harvest, *is the kind of work better served on the page — and which it should never have left. Highly derivative, the play is wordy and self-indulgent; nothing much happens. The author's focus seems not to be on the experience of the audience (or even his characters) but his own gratification, never mind that this leads us to something disappointingly shallow — and clearly not written with care nor edited with rigour.*

"To be fair there is a modicum of interest in the character of the farmer, but the German pilot is little more than a Baron von Richthofen cliché, and the interaction between the two is trite. Given so much great and reflective work has been produced during and since the war — and thus could have provided Charles E. with much to be mined — it is a shame he appears not to have done so, but rather has chosen to skip superficially across the subject's surface like a stone skimming on a lake.

"If Tainted Harvest *was well-received (and in some quarters it seemed to be) then perhaps others saw merit in it which escaped this reviewer."*

~

We had exams in June; exams that counted, were important. In total, I think they made up about a third of our overall grade — and there were no second chances. You couldn't secure a final classification through them, but you could cock them up well enough to ensure you'd fail to get what had been predicted no matter how hard you worked in the final year. Because two of the modules weren't my strongest — Shakespeare and the Romantics — I had no choice but to knuckle down; and knuckling down meant spending less time writing creatively. In fact I wrote hardly anything that May and June.

Across that same period The Hive changed too, transformed from an intensely creative weekly workout, a thrashing of ideas, a cauldron of experimentation, to more of an oasis of calm. It was where some of us went to relieve the pressure. Not surprisingly numbers dropped during those two months, and those of us who continued to turn up merely wanted a quiet haven where we didn't have to think about *King Lear* or Shelley.

As you might imagine, the combination of exams and a muted Hive derailed creative output for most people. Once exams were over many were off on their holidays, and when they returned in September a few couldn't be bothered to re-engage. That was another reason the numbers of third-year attendees always fell away. For me, those two exam months also acted as a firebreak from the trauma I'd been putting myself through post-Horberry. In writing next to nothing, I had very little about which I could crucify myself — though I should admit that my new-found editing skills had proved a boon for two final assignments: essays on 'The Short Story' and 'The War Poets'.

When July came round and we were released from exams it felt as if I was starting again.

And I almost was. It was another summer of visiting friends and sofa-surfing; a summer spent trying to relocate my mojo, the one which had spawned *Tainted Harvest*. If it too had absconded for the holidays no-one was more surprised than me, especially as I actually wrote an enormous amount — though mainly starting new things I didn't finish or which left me feeling pitifully inadequate. I tried revisiting some old tried-and-tested themes too, if only to see whether I could recover any sense of who I was.

People talk about 'finding your voice'. This was something you never consider when you're being continually propelled forward by a wave of trial, error, and modest success. Any inkling I may have had which suggested that I'd lost it (my voice, that is) was — at one level — entirely misplaced: how could you lose something you'd never found?

It was a summer I'd assumed would be about me getting back into the flow — only to discover that there was no flow to get back into.

- Don't you think you're being a little harsh on yourself?

I did find some new voices of a sort though. I started to curate internal conversations along the way contemporaneous with events — a habit I now find resurfacing as part of this process; virtual encounters in my head to keep me company.

Maybe it was (or is) needing a sounding board, something to challenge me or as a means to verify some hypotheses or other. Mainly it was Matty who was chivvying me along. Even if he was occasionally abrasive, I looked out for those moments when he was trying to be constructive, positive. Sometimes the voice belonged to someone else, when I needed to give myself a different kind of message. However, it was never Horberry nor Martha — hardly a surprise! It wasn't even Valerie or Jack; maybe that says something about what I thought they could offer me. Sometimes the voice was Whitehurst or a Chorus-like figure, but of course the whispering was me all along. Doesn't everyone do that?

These days it's only ever Matty.

- You thought I was 'abrasive'? [You can see how the conversations might have gone.] You were still a kid really. Give yourself a break.

- You may be eternally trapped in being a kid, brother mine, but some of us have moved on, grown up.

- Is that what you call it?

Of course I can't recall those original conversations, the exact words from 1970. Certainly not. Indeed, there weren't really words at all; not vocalised, at any rate. So you'll have to cut me some slack with this 'reimagining'. Let's call it 'artistic licence'.

In spite of what I've just said about July and August, across those couple of months — gradually, unconsciously — something began to surface. At first what I was drafting felt no more than a mash-up of everything I'd written before (I mean, how could it not!), but by the first week in September I began to get a sense of a new tone, a different undercurrent. It may have been no more than a glimmer. If I had to equate it with anything it was a little like a tuning fork beginning to find its note, a purer sound piercing the cacophony. Sounds a bit over-blown — but it's better than some hackneyed phrase about things appearing through a fog…

There were two triggers. The first was a poem — 'Skipton' — which I wrote between Leeds and Manchester that August. Wanting to test it out, I entered it into a competition (something I rarely did then and now never do) and it ended up being 'highly commended'. You may know it. The second was a *very* short story written from a prompt I found somewhere. Or it might have been born from something I saw in the paper, or a sudden impulse arriving out-of-the-blue as I was walking down the road. 'Downsizing'. You may know that too; God knows I've read it often enough at events!

So there they were. Modest epiphanies if you like. Either the beginnings of a new voice or the resurrection of an old one. You choose.

- New voice. That's what you've always said.

- Who asked you?

In many respects what that period represented — especially July and August — was a reset followed by a subconscious curating of the best bits from the previous eighteen months' experience. More than that, I now believe the cornerstones of my modest reinvention (if I can call it that) was the rigour I'd been forced to apply to my work. Not merely because of Imogen and Horberry, but academically via the tutors, and perhaps through others in The Hive too. The bar had gradually been getting higher, the heads of the Hydra harder to reach, never mind slice off.

What else?

Was I a changed person in consequence?

Come October I was once more comfortable leading The Hive, 'first amongst equals'; and I was three-parts of the way through a play, *Frigid Air*, that the Drama Group said they wanted to put on at the end of term. Recalling what had happened the previous December, in some senses the offer was almost a reprise. Or a reprieve. So I was back on track. Or in a new and improved groove.

~

JOSH   And?

RYAN   What do you mean: 'and'?

JOSH   Jesus! [*exasperated*] Afterwards. After you left the concert, left the bar, went back to her hall, what happened then? I wasn't expecting to see you until lunchtime today at the earliest, not sitting here before ten having breakfast!

RYAN gets up from the table and walks over to the sink where he fills the kettle, switches it on.

JOSH   Well?

RYAN   She made coffee. We talked for a while — about the concert, books, her family. Then I walked back here. About one thirty it must have been.

JOSH   You walked back here?! Did she throw you out? Did you embarrass yourself? Lizzie's quite a girl — and what's more, she likes you. A lot. Though fucked if I know why! And now she's probably changed her mind after your non-performance last night.

RYAN   [*sitting back down*] Why should she have?

JOSH   Listen to yourself. Don't you have any idea?

RYAN   We had a really nice time. The band was great.

JOSH   Okay, I'll buy that — but didn't you make a move? Did she want you to or not?

RYAN stands and walks to the front of the stage; addresses the audience.

RYAN   There was a moment when she reclined on the sofa... I was transfixed by the shape of her mouth, the buttons on her shirt. She'd laughed at something I'd said, then laid back. I knew what she was saying; it was a wordless invitation. All I had to do was to lean forward and kiss her. And that was what I wanted more than anything else — but I was paralysed. I couldn't move. After a minute, maybe less, she sat back up and the moment was gone...and now I know there'll never be another. Not with Lizzie. But how can I tell Josh all that?

RYAN returns to the kettle and switches it off; takes a mug from the cupboard. Begins to prepare his coffee.

RYAN   It wasn't like that.

~

You can call that finding a new voice if you want to (as I think I did for a while) but it was closer to relocating myself, hunting down my mojo, reaffirming the course I was setting out for myself.

It turned out the May/June exams had gone well. Heading into my final year I was pretty certain of at least an Upper Second. Frank told me I could still get a First. In a bizarre echo of Whitehurst, he said *You'll need to work for it*, yet all the while knowing I wouldn't, that my ambitions lay elsewhere. He talked about 'balance' — which was code for spending less time on the non-academic stuff. I smiled at him. He knew what that meant too.

- You'd become arrogant, big-headed.

- Oh, I don't think so. Confident and surer of foot perhaps; a little more certain of where I was headed.

- You thought you were becoming immortal, unbeatable. Come that November it was as if Horberry had never existed.

- Oh he'd existed all right! I had the scars to prove it. Still do.

- We could debate that.

- There's no point. You know I'd win.

That's what fighting battles does, isn't it? Toughens you up; teaches you what works and what doesn't. You learn how to win.

- If you want to put it that way, in such combative terms.

- I can answer my own questions, thank you.

I *was* a changed person. When 1970 dawned I was twenty-one, I'd been at university for two-and-a-half years — and away from home that long too. I'd written two plays that had been performed, and dozens of stories and poems. I was running a writing group and had a decent academic record. I'd been challenged, criticised, knocked down. And I'd got back up.

How could I not be different?

- And you'd served your self-imposed sentence?

- Along the way, some of it, yes.

- Really?

- As if you didn't know that I'm still serving it still...

At that moment it wasn't about the past. It was a new year, a new decade. Wasn't everyone looking forward? Yes, there were those who knew what they were heading towards: teacher training, post-grad, graduate programmes with multi-nationals. I had none of that. Compared to them, my future was empty, uncertain.

Yet because of this it was also better than theirs. Immeasurably. My future would be decided by the words I would continue to put together, one after the other; I would craft my future myself. Pick any term you want, but I would *build* my life. After *Frigid Air*, well... That Christmas was — luxurious. I revelled in the certainty of what lay ahead.

- You could foresee it?

- Don't be ridiculous! Of course I couldn't.

In the same way that no-one can possibly know which word will follow the last one they wrote or the one after that, I had no idea about the next month, the next week. Even the next day! I knew it wouldn't be plain sailing; I'd already experience enough to know that. But I was ready.

- Were you? Really?

- I told myself I was. Isn't that half the battle?

- Is it? You tell me. You're the other side of it now. Your precious 'future' — the future you denied me — has become your past; so weigh it up, make the judgement call.

- All I know is that I felt powerful. I'd been in fights and survived. I'd learned lessons and survived.

- Fights! You were still a kid.

I didn't need to be told that. By anyone. Then or now.

So was I ready?

Not in a million years.

Hind

1971 - 1976

I suppose I should talk about love.

I've not really mentioned it thus far, preferring the more rudimentary signifier 'sex' and leaving it up to you to interpret, decipher, add your own meaning. The word's physicality, if you will. And what you may have come up with has nothing at all to do with me, of course; you will have settled on a fiction aligned to your own dreams and desires, your own set of lies. *Your* fantasies, not mine.

Having said that, the distance between your imaginings and my truth may not be that great. At least in one or two instances. But if you think I'm going to give you chapter and verse simply for your lewd satisfaction, spelling out the minutiae of all my encounters… Well, think again.

'No names, no pack-drill'. Not that I've a clue what that really means.

Let's just say I was a 'healthy' young man. Is that enough? Or are you made in the Horberry mould and would like a little more in terms of trite cliché. If I might occasionally choose to indulge you just a touch, don't make the mistake of assuming that I actually care about what you think. Was I 'indiscriminate'? Possibly. 'Unfaithful'? At least once. 'Cruel?'

I would want to push back at cruel. It was never my intention to be so. Interpretation, obviously. If I was 'honest' — at least in my own eyes — then I'm prepared to concede how some episodes might have been regarded negatively if viewed through an alternate lens.

People like the notion of 'lenses' these days, don't they? Offers such opportunities for excuses. Or lies.

Don't think all of the above is irrelevant when it comes to talking about love. We only truly know what a thing is when we know what it *isn't*. Night has no meaning without day, light without dark. And love needs the context of not-love perhaps manifest not through hate but rather an identical physical experience tainted with an alternative underlying motivation and perspective. How coy is that?!

Another 'lens', of course.

Had I been in love during my three years in Sheffield? No, certainly not. Oh, I might have imagined so at the time, besotted by the notion of it, swept along by the general search for it, seduced by its promise — but that would have been akin to falling for 'smooth' without knowing what 'rough' felt like. The day/night, light/dark thing. I see that now. Or saw it soon enough. It's easy to get sucked in, isn't it; to think you're 'in love'. And those Byronesque-types, the boys who wanted to be poets, they were in love all the time; hardly a day went by when they weren't in anguish over some girl. Or some other boy in one or two cases — though back then such liaisons were far less prevalent. Or public. Maybe both. We had one openly gay lecturer who was hardly a positive role model if you were that way inclined. His pantomime-like faux-femininity was more antidote than inspiration.

Given my background up to that point — experiencing sex without any serious connection — love wasn't something I'd really thought about, considered, aspired to; at least not outside the literary, the theoretical. I was happy enough with my own private interpretation. I had no doubt that there existed something other, something deeper and far more meaningful, but it wasn't on my radar. Which also meant I felt it difficult to write about. Perhaps *Frigid Air* exposed that. I'll admit that my approach to love/sex could — on reflection — be considered self-centred, transactional, concrete; but it was never dishonest. Or cruel. Not to my mind.

Does that offer redemption, if redemption is needed? You'll have your own view. Anyway, as if in retribution or to balance the scales, I learned what cruel was soon enough.

When I met Hazel Lockwood I was twenty-two and recently released from the structure of university. No more lectures, no more timetable, no more Hive. Cut loose. Or abandoned. Some of my erstwhile student acquaintances attached themselves to new lives soon enough: a few went into teacher training (whether they were suited to the profession or not); a couple stayed on to study for a Master's and delay the evil day when academia would spit them out. Those who were more flexible — and perhaps less emotionally committed to the subject that had dominated the last three years of their lives — were happy to accept basement-level jobs or internships in insurance companies, banks, multi-nationals, government. One was parachuted into the world of 'the family firm' and set for life.

And me?

With my future decided (in that I remained convinced I *would* be a successful writer!) all I needed to do was find a modest income where the work didn't demand too much of me mentally, settle on a location which offered some of the cultural benefits befitting a city, and live in a place where I could write. A new city, a new life, another start; and remember, it was also the dawning of a new decade.

Lincoln seemed a reasonable bet. Although the county town, it wasn't on the scale of many larger cities — which was appealing given my experience of the less salubrious areas of Sheffield. There was no university (though one would receive its charter sixteen years later) but there *were* colleges, a night-life of sorts, a bustling town centre, plus the cathedral, a castle, museums and art galleries… The mix was attractive. The two part-time jobs I secured — one in a bookshop, the other in the Usher Gallery (in spite of my knowledge being limited to what I'd learned at A-level) — were sufficient to fund a small one-bedroom top floor flat in a low-grade conversion on the 'wrong' side of town not far from the station. More importantly, they allowed me time enough to devote to my writing. Within a few weeks I'd begun to settle into a new routine: work, writing, domestic necessities. In many respects, it wasn't that far removed from university.

And it was onto this oddly haphazard scaffolding that Hazel climbed one day.

Early September. I'd been in Lincoln for a couple of months by then. Still feeling the loss of The Hive and all it had offered, one of the first things I'd done was to seek out a local writing group. The one I chose met once a fortnight in a pub near the cathedral; a dark and somewhat damp room occupied for three hours on alternate Wednesday evenings. It was free-of-charge on the understanding that members would buy drinks when they were there. The pub was always dead on a Wednesday; no darts or pool matches. My first attendance was probably at the beginning of August. The meeting turnout was disappointing. *It's because of the holidays* someone said, clearly amazed that the summer had foisted a new member on them (i.e. me).

After the experience of The Hive — and my role within it — I remember being generally non-plussed at a gathering which seemed more intent on drinking than writing. Members who'd been attending for many years were its ringleaders, steering the meetings the way they had always been steered, running the group the way it had always been run. I can't recall much about the first three meetings, only the growing sense that I'd made a tactical mistake and needed to reverse myself out of there as soon as I possibly could.

Hazel and two others pitched up during the mid-September session; they were greeted like returning prophets. All three were students now embarking on their final year's study at the local college, and while none were English majors (being variously devoted to other flavours of the Humanities) they had attended the group for most of their time in the city. Theirs was an arrival which invested our cabal with some much needed energy and, by the middle of October, things were looking a little brighter. Okay, it wasn't The Hive, but it seemed it might turn out not to be the dead-end I'd feared.

I recognise now that my judgement, that reassessment, may have been clouded. How could it not have been? If I wanted to be harsh I could categorise our collective as a sad little gathering largely devoid of any meaningful talent and ambition; an excuse for a writing group with some of its members being oddly pathetic individuals. Yet Hazel's presence meant it was improper to regard it in such a fashion, to tar everyone with the same brush. Had I done so I would have followed through on my plan to leave — but leaving would have meant not seeing Hazel again.

As far as I can recall, her sudden appearance gave rise to the first ever instance when I relegated my writing to second place. And it was the first time I'd ever felt something which teetered beyond lust.

Hazel was slim and pretty; in fact she reminded me of Donna Reed from my mother's favourite film, *It's a Wonderful Life*. A Christmas staple for all my eleven years with her and Jack, I had been bored by it, never able to see beyond the schmaltz. Yet it wasn't Hazel's prettiness which drew me in. She was attentive, enthusiastic, clearly intelligent, perceptive, and her critiquing was always delivered considerately and earnestly. And although what she wrote had little merit (as she herself confessed!) she seemed to like my work. Imogen but with a different soul perhaps. Not that I believe in people having 'souls'.

Drawn together, we found ourselves sitting next to each other in meetings, lingering over a final drink at the end of a session. There were increasingly frequent comings-together at other times, other evenings. The odd lunch or weekend walk. I confess to being lost — and lost in a way that was entirely new to me. At times I even saw myself gravitating towards the adoption of one of those Byronesque personalities! Perhaps I understood them for the first time.

On the one hand my writing suffered (there was a less of it), but on the other I found myself exploring themes that were entirely new to me. Themes and emotions. Oh, I had written about 'love' before — how could I not have done? — but never with an 'insider's' view.

Whatever Hazel's feelings were during those autumn months I never discovered. Or rather, I only got an insight into them much later. My own inclination probably being painfully self-evident, it was during one of our weekend walks (as I remember it, in the somewhat shabby city centre arboretum cowering in early winter cold) that she told me about her recent break-up, how she had been shattered by her ex-boyfriend's infidelity, and how it would take her time to mend. When I suggested that — based on how she came across in the writing group — it was impossible to tell she was suffering, she laughed and said she'd always been a good actress. Donna Reed. Again.

Her message — delivered in response to an unasked question — was all too plain. As was my choice. Should I abandon the group and abandon Hazel; move on, and put my writing back on its rightful pedestal? Yet — Byronesque or not — how could I? The only real option was to continue to endure the group for the reward of spending time with her — and in doing so, suffer the anguish of waiting; cultivate patience in the hope that there would come a time when I would be rewarded.

And I was. Many months later.

If I was to be honest (and if I can't be honest here, where can I be?!) I was half-expecting my feelings for Hazel to wane, to be swamped by an ever-increasing frustration with the group — and a desperation to be writing more. But the opposite happened. I became more determined, more resolute. It was a resolution which saw me try all sorts of things to make the group palatable: I led the odd session; pushed boundaries where I could; varied my approach in terms of being enthusiastic or critical of the work shared there. Hazel could see what was going on. An occasional private smile was all it took for her to demonstrate she could see right through me.

At the end of the first meeting after her final exams, she took my hand and said *Don't you think it's about time I saw your flat?* I collapsed — if not physically, then at least mentally. Wasn't that exactly what was supposed to happen?

Being both completely victorious *and* utterly defeated at the same time was a blend which forced Hazel to steer us through the next few days; to get me back to something approaching normal, like a pilot helping navigate a ship through a narrow channel. 'Something approaching normal'? No; it was a *new* normal. Arrival at a longed-for destination; the end of a mammoth journey, like Odysseus perhaps. I would wake up in the mornings with her at my side (*my* Penelope) and feel as if I had slipped through to some parallel universe.

And the world was changed too. My writing suddenly pivoted and I rediscovered something unnameable I hadn't realised was missing. I became re-engaged, energised; ideas began to flow, Hazel having released them.

No; that's not correct either. Rather, it was as if, in finally securing our relationship, *I* had been able to free those ideas, to loose the chains; as if *I* had been bottling-up my creativity, conning myself into mediocrity by choosing to be satisfied with visits to an insignificant and second-rate writing group, one that was little more than a placebo. Or even less than that. I was twenty-three and re-born; Hazel had been released from her course. And we celebrated our freedom by tying ourselves together.

Twenty-three.

Given the spin I'd been in, I'm not sure I really knew what I was doing. Nor what I was going to do. My life seemed to be split in two: the intellectual part which was dominated by my course, and the wreckage of the emotional part I had been clinging to. There was little room for anything else. Against that backdrop, is it any wonder that when my course finished I used that as a trigger to try and shake myself emotionally? It was a 'clearing of the decks', a sweeping away with 'a new broom' — all those kinds of tired clichés — and in doing so I found myself strangely free, intellectually and emotionally. Or at least that's what I thought.

Perhaps it was a state for which I'd longed. Perhaps I'd assumed that, in consequence, I would be propelled into a new world, a refreshed existence where I could re-find myself. Yet it seemed as if I'd walked into a void; where there had once been order — the intellectual — and disorder — the emotional — there was now nothing. I knew I had a rare opportunity to build something from scratch, that I could take my time to define what I wanted my future to look like, but the void scared me; I'd thrown myself into it without any kind of safety net.

Maybe that's what Charles was — or why I chose to adopt him. A safety net. Here was man about my age who could not only satisfy me intellectually but also come to my rescue emotionally, even if I had no idea to what extent he might do so. As a writer he was clearly talented (though in the circles in which we moved the competition wasn't exactly strong!), and it was painfully evident he liked me. I was presented with an opportunity to save myself from the void by making a single choice: Charles was the knight in shining armour who could slay both intellectual and emotional dragons. Given I had stared into an abyss which had no form, no content, no boundaries, how could I not take a chance on the remediation he might be able to offer me?

I would be lying if I didn't confess to moments in those early Lincoln days when I looked back at my life with wonder, slightly in awe at how much I'd managed to fill it with — or how much I'd had forced upon me. Control and no control. It felt as if I'd lived three lives already: my life as a child; one as an burgeoning writer; and now something else. My life with Hazel. Although I knew this new incarnation was different — that things would be altered from then on — I struggled to foresee exactly how the change might manifest itself. Because of that, I chose not to give it a name nor assign it any privileged status even though I sensed it was 'special'.

Not that it was, of course. Not really. People are falling into and out of love all the time. There is nothing remarkable about attachment. At least not in the sense of its profligacy. All I was doing was behaving normally, submitting myself to one of the great joys of life.

And it *was* a joy, being with Hazel. Half of 'a couple'. And writing again. We redefined ourselves against this new normal: emotionally, domestically, creatively. Even though she kept her own digs to ensure she had 'a space' — *temporarily, in case I need it* — she pretty much lived with me in my little flat, getting herself a temporary job in Boots' *while we sort ourselves out*.

That was the next question of course. I had examined my past, but I was now also interrogating my future too, our future; for how could it not be something with Hazel in it, centred around her and my writing? Yet as we settled into our new conjoined existence, and as my writing began to bloom again (we stopped going to the insipid writing group!), 'the future' somehow failed to solidify, remaining vague and mirage-like. In spite of there being no change in work — Hazel in Boots', me in the gallery, the bookshop — I managed to resurrect the old certainty that I *would* be a successful writer and tried to use that as my North Star. It was ploy which was only partially effective because 'being a writer' could now only consume half the person I was fast becoming. Did I ever ask myself whether half of me would be enough?

I remembered Imogen and Horberry. I remembered criticism. I recognised how part of being a writer was being challenged, told you were unworthy. And, less frequently, being told that you were good. How that contradiction made you stronger. How it demanded every morsel of you. And I couldn't help but wonder not only where my next critics might come from, but whether love — like writing — also needed a counterpoint; that there might be, waiting invisibly in the wings, an equivalence, a disruptor, something to unpick the new existence in which I had so wholeheartedly invested.

The present was wonderful — but gradually I came to fear the future.

~

Less than three years later I discovered that future had a name: Kieran Millar. It was a future with a past too; Hazel's past. Millar had been the one who had cheated on her — and who (as it turned out) was also unable to forget her. Hazel having freed herself of him, Millar discovered the reverse fixture was unplayable.

To the best of my knowledge he left her alone for nearly two years until he saw her one day in Boots'. Unexpected moments like that can knock you off your stride, skittle you sideways. Whether or not that was what happened in Millar's case I've no idea. You'd have to ask him. And her. But he managed to wheedle his way back in — presumably by being profusely apologetic — and begged (I'm guessing here) for them to be friends again. Hazel not being a hard-edged soul, I can see how she would have opened the door just a little rather than slam it in his face. Was it a year later — almost as long as I had waited for her — she eventually capitulated? Or less? However long it took him to re-establish himself in her affections (or for her to give in), the subsequent breach could only leave me stunned.

I guess I've always loved him she said, as if disqualifying anything she felt for me, relegating it to some subordinate division. *And these days you're spending so much of your time writing…* Even if I'd acknowledged that as true (and it was) there was no way it qualified as a capital offence. Surely. I thought my life was in balance; I believed I'd attained some kind of nirvana: writer and lover coexisting in perfect equilibrium. But what *I* thought suddenly ceased to matter. It was what Hazel thought that counted. Perhaps Millar had been whispering in her ear, taking advantage of the hours I assume he must have spent in 'her space', the space for which she'd found a recycled use, clandestine or otherwise.

Was it ironic that, having taken so long to build my new life, it should be decimated so quickly? One difficult conversation, one painful evening, and it was all over. I'd had the heart ripped out of me. It was as if the emotional equivalent of Horberry had turned up on my doorstep and announced that, all this time, I'd been working in completely the wrong language.

But I didn't believe it then, and I don't believe it now. I hadn't misinterpreted what I felt. More than that — and as ridiculous as it may sound — I decided I wouldn't let those feelings be corrupted, that I could never replicate what I'd had with Hazel, that even trying to do so would be terminal. So they needed to be preserved, like specimens in a jar.

Looking back now? Now it's too late? Hokum, probably. 'Romantic' with a capital R.

And in any event, isn't it always too late?

You might ask if I forgave her — God knows enough people have! — and my response has always been the same: there was nothing to forgive. There was pain, yes — as there had been with Martha and Imogen and Horberry, various flavours

of the stuff — but with pain comes instruction, education; and
if you choose to regard those lessons as central to your being,
your future life, then what is there to forgive? Forgiveness
suggests you wish something had never happened, and that
you would have preferred to remain innocent. Or that you're
weak.

Of course I could just as easily have killed that bastard Millar.

~

*For a while it worked, Charles and I. I felt like a child who was
learning how to ride a bike and this nice man had suddenly
arrived on the scene with a pair of stabilisers.*

*Leaving the writing group and striking out on our own had an
immediate positive impact, especially for Charles. And while I
continued to occasionally work on my own bits and pieces, I
had no problem being in his shadow. And our emotional life
blossomed too. He was — I could see — ridiculously happy;
and I revelled in the security inherited from his presence,
knowing how he felt about me, how invested he was in what we
might become.*

Or at least that was how it seemed.

*And then I came to realise that I was subservient in ways I
hadn't expected. Not the practical or domestic — we both
worked, earned our pittance, contributed to the everyday cost of
our existence together — but emotionally and intellectually. I
discovered I'd swapped one kind of void for another.*

*In comparison to his writing, I was the poor relation; not only
was my work second class, but in consequence he somehow
came to make me feel second class too. And as for emotional
rewards, Charles always put himself first. Oh, he talked about
'us' and we discussed an imagined future, but such things were
always on his terms, measured against his criteria. Rather than
a partner, I began to feel as if I was more a facilitator or a*

supplier; I was there to meet his needs, not to satisfy my own. Hence the re-opening void.

This was something I'd never felt with Kieran. Indeed our relationship had — in many ways — been the opposite; and although he'd been a bastard and unpicked what we'd had, I couldn't help but feel that for much of the time I'd at least been on a par, the emotional rewards shared equitably. His sudden reappearance, tail between his legs like a guilt-ridden puppy, happened to coincide with the beginning of my questioning of where I was going with Charles and what our future might look like. Kieran gave me something to hold up to the light and which offered a comparison with where I currently was and where I was heading.

You might say there were risks attached to both prospects, and you'd be right; but the dichotomy between the known — how Kieran was — and the unknown — what the future with Charles might look like — loomed ever larger.

It was another choice, and one which took me many weeks to resolve; and all the while I was teasing at both options, trying to flesh them out. A certain duplicity was needed on my part to hold them both in balance. That isn't something of which I'm proud; indeed I wasn't proud of it then, but it was a necessary weighing of how I might best survive.

There was never any doubt Charles would be devastated. Or that he would assume he was devastated. I have seen and heard things over the years; things he has said or written, about me, our life together. And much of it is true. Indeed, I would be lying if I hadn't — from time to time — imagined what my life would have been like had I stayed with him. And how <u>his</u> life would have turned out, for surely there would have been some difference.

If my abandoning him led him to write some of the things he did (this is my attempt to rationalise or process what happened)

~

Was there something else though? I know that's what you're
thinking. That perhaps there's something I'm not telling you.
I'm sure the more Mills & Boon-inclined of you would like to
believe I got my own back on Millar, that at some point I
cuckolded *him*, won Hazel back. Or that Hazel was mentally
sick and I eventually rescued her for good. And you might
feel justified in that conjecture if you assumed the subsequent
narrative has been deliberately kept outside of the public
domain; Hazel's and my secret. Romance and secrecy: is there
a headier mix?

Well, believe it if you want to. There would have been a time
when I wished it so.

Alternatively you might like to imagine that Hazel became a
'Muse', installed on a pedestal up to which I could look in
order to garner inspiration; that she became some kind of
beacon, or paragon, or untouchable goddess. I can't stop you
believing that either — even if it's only marginally closer to
the truth.

The truth?

We were both young; still kids, really. She was — in my eyes
at least — beautiful, mesmeric, enchanting. I fell head-over-
heels, unable to stop myself. I was patient. Then for a couple
of years we fucked like rabbits, talked about the future,
dreamed up scenarios of how life might be. I wrote and was
happy.

Then her past caught up with her — or my future caught up
with me. You choose. She fucked more, I fucked less. That

was about the size of it before the whole house-of-cards collapsed.

Is that crude enough for you? Rudimentary? Explicit? Clear?

And I carry those three years with me as I have always carried them; how can I not? But it's more than that isn't it? I'm not talking about memory or anything so superficial, sentimental or slushy. Hazel was like a blood transfusion; she swept through every part of me, merging herself with my very atoms. Having done so — and thus continuing to do so forever — she found a way to infuse my writing too. Every single sentence I have ever written since then has had her touch upon it.

Which, I suppose, is one reason I never looked for 'Hazel, mark-II'; there wouldn't have been capacity for the contribution of a second 'true love' in my words! Imagine the in-fighting! And don't forget, it's not just Hazel who inhabits them. Martha's there, seeping through; and Valerie and Matty; Imogen and Horberry. That's the writer's curse. Whether we wish to or not, whether we recognise it or not, we become the compound voice comprising everyone who has ever touched us. Everyone. We are never, ever, pure. Even those first words we write — maybe even the first ones we babble — are already tainted by others.

On that basis you might argue that I have no words of my own. Perhaps that's why we write and search, write and search, hoping one day to find some. Or maybe just one. That might be enough.

~

That's bollocks! I hear some future version of you claiming, even *before* you've read those words (given that I've only just written them). They represent — you may say — nothing more than the fabrication of an excuse, an abdication, the passing off of my failures as the fault of others.

I've heard it all before, and if you think it's true then, like everyone else, you're just plain wrong. You simply don't understand. If you don't write, how can you? There's a cacophony in my head *all the time;* an orchestra of voices and ideas and memories all vying for primacy, all wanting 'out', to be spoken, to be listened to. I am no more than the vehicle for them. Or perhaps I'm akin to the poor driver of a school bus filled with rowdy kids, the only one who's trying to retain sufficient attention to keep the damn vehicle on the road.

Do you know what that's like?

How can you?

The other claim — which became insidiously and increasingly prevalent, especially when it was far too late for me to disprove it (in any sense!) — was that I 'have a problem with women'. Thinking they're being original, some people (many who should know better!) have trotted out a list of flawed relationships — my mother, Martha, Imogen, Hazel, all the others — as if doing so is super-clever or proof of something profound. Of my 'problem' I suppose. And then they pontificate about the emotions with which I supposedly struggle — like attachment and 'love' — and associate those emotions with the aforementioned individuals as if that's supposed to 'seal the deal'.

What do you expect me to say? That I don't have a problem? Or that I do? Or that all men have exactly the same problem?

Sometimes answers are irrelevant, whether they're right or wrong.

Women have provided me with the framework for my life. Is that more acceptable, appropriate? Would you 'buy' that? They have been there at pivotal points, those of flux or intersection. Or they are the giant stones set in the earth which make up my own personal Stonehenge — and the monument they create is me.

Surely that's writerly enough for you!

Even I would have to admit there's something of the truth buried in there, flowery or otherwise. Lessons. Emotions and lessons. Isn't it through emotion that you learn about abandonment and love and betrayal and pragmatism? Like complex algebra, you have to be taught how to solve it — and you're only ready to learn once you have an understanding of the basic concepts.

One plus one; everything stems from that.

People — and yes, perhaps in my case, especially women — have been the great educators. Oh, you learn from men too. It's clear that I discovered things through Jack say, or Hamer. Horberry. Even Millar. But weren't those more rudimentary and practical, the craft-related, the everyday? Weren't the 'big ticket' items exposed by the women in my life?

You can see it in my writing. I didn't write anything meaningful about women — or write much about women at all in fact — until after Hazel. That should be confession enough.

She's in my atoms, like I say.

And before you claim that's all too neat, too 'pat', then allow me to put a hole in your balloon before you even try and inflate it. That's my truth: a statement of debt, not a laying of blame. And frankly whether you believe me or not is strangely neither here nor there. My history, my words.

We're all translators in our own way.

Boar

1970 - 1980

And you're spending so much of your time writing these days she had said. When had I not been? In the context of my work there was no pre- and post-Hazel, not really. Or if there was, it was in subject matter only; not in the act, the heinous act of writing.

If you were desperate to locate where anything actually and meaningfully changed, how far would you want to go back? Is there a base camp? I've always thought of *Tainted Harvest* as a good marker. Before and after. But not really in the sense of process; please understand that. It was a locus from an entirely different register. Yes, *Tainted Harvest* was in part an exercise to prove that I could do something substantial, but after that — emboldened, if you like — most times I just wanted to do something *hard*.

Perhaps that's what this is.

It would have been all too easy to have trotted out the same thing over and over again, *Tainted Harvest Redux*. A common enough trap; you see it everywhere. There were those in The Hive who, irrespective of prompt or theme or challenge, produced identical drivel week in, week out. As if they'd found something magical, too good to let go. Which they hadn't. On the other hand, I knew I was still in the foothills of finding my 'voice'; there was more exploring to be done, and yes, some failures to be endured.

Of course, I can afford to say that now, looking back. I'm secure enough in my position; I have the evidence, the legacy to admit such a navel-gazing preoccupation may have existed — even if it hadn't. Even if I thought...

Anyway, enough.

In addition to Frank, we had a professor — Jensen, a Dane from Copenhagen — who occasionally taught modernism. He loved Joyce too, and had written introductions for Danish editions of *Dubliners* and *Portrait*. I once asked him how popular Danish translations were. It was a dumb question he chose not to answer. I felt my card being marked.

It was coming up to Easter in my second year. He took a couple of tutorials on *Ulysses*, and at the end of the first of these set an essay on the 'Penelope' section — but gave us less than a week to write it. The guidelines were slack; something about arguing whether or not the form helped or hindered the narrative. Bread-and-butter stuff really, with only one logical conclusion to be drawn. Or one we students were expected to draw. There were eight of us in the group, and I was convinced he would be rewarded with eight pretty much identical essays.

Which is why I chose to write mine in its own form of stream of consciousness. I did so not only to mimic 'Penelope' and its narrative, but to *really* use the form to support my argument — even weaving in quotes from the novel itself, as if I'd written it and not Joyce. I wanted to see how much I could blur everything: the original text, the analysis, the style, the academic argument. It was to be a cohesive piece, a 'mind-dump' encapsulating everything.

That was what made it extra hard. The first challenge was to write the thing in just a few days; the second was to make it work in an academic frame of reference.

He handed the essays back at the end of the next tutorial. All except mine. He kept me back for that, one-to-one.

I'm giving you two marks, Charles he said; *the first is a mark for your essay as academic endeavour — and I'm failing it.* Then, before I could protest, *But as a piece of creative writing, it's one of the most remarkable things I've ever seen a student produce.*

We were allowed to drop three pieces each year from the continual assessment which made up part of our final degree. I dropped that essay — even though I thought it probably the best thing I'd ever produced.

- I doubt it.

- What do you know about it, you weren't there.

- You're just trumpet-blowing knowing there's no-one who can judge, to validate what Jensen did or did not say.

- Meaning?

- He might just have failed you. That bit about "one of the most remarkable things" could be nothing more than fabrication, a confection to sweeten the episode.

- "A confection"? That's pretty good.

- Coming from me, you mean?

- Not at all. Just pretty good. I might use it. 'Confection' is such a lovely word, don't you think?

Matty didn't answer. How could he?

~

Ignoring *Frigid Air*, my second major confection (see what I did there!) was also a stage play. Why not, given the success of *Tainted Harvest*?

Let me locate the chronology of it for you. It was post-University and before my 'formal' relationship with Hazel i.e. in that twilight zone of creativity during my first year living in Lincoln.

The wife of someone at the writing group (I forget her name) was a member of a local drama outfit. Nothing outstanding, it had a small local following and access to a couple of venues where they performed three or four times a year, mainly to modest audiences consisting of friends, family, students, and the odd academic. They were looking for something for Easter. 1972 it would have been. I told them about *Tainted Harvest*; said I was looking for a project. And I was. At that point I'd been working on various bits and pieces, nothing material. They seemed interested.

Rightly or wrongly, I had no doubt I'd be able to repeat the success of my first play.

- Of course!

- Call it the folly of youth.

- If you like.

I knew where the play would be put on — an intimate space which meant whatever I wrote had to be small scale — and I knew when they'd want to start rehearsals. Although there were perhaps ten of them in the group, I'd been casually informed that only three or four could really act, so that also provided a constraint — after all I didn't want my words butchered by some ham!

The challenge was subject matter.

If it was going to be worth tackling it had to be difficult. And not just for me in terms of the writing, but for the audience too. I didn't want people leaving the theatre feeling warm and fuzzy, merely having had a good time. I wanted them to go home thinking about what they'd seen and heard, asking questions of themselves.

So I chose rape.

You won't be surprised to know I used my mother's history for the background. Or what little I knew of it. Early on in the drafting process I decided I'd start the play with the scene of the rape itself. I'd smack the audience right between the eyes from curtain up. There would be no 'getting comfy'. The first thing the lead female actor did would not be to speak but to scream.

When it came to the first read-through some of the company weren't keen; but the three leads (including the wife of the guy from the writing group) not only recognised the merit in the play, but also the acting challenges it would present.

It wasn't a pantomime, after all!

But then you probably already know something about *Sunbathing*: the story of how a man is tormented by the sight of a young woman he regularly sees sunbathing on Brighton beach. Importantly, she is not seen 'innocently' but observed through a telescope bought for exactly that purpose, one he has set-up in the window of his seafront flat… Voyeurism. You get the idea. Like *Tainted Harvest*, the stage was split in two: half was his flat and half the beach. After the rape scene (in his flat) the play is in two parts; the first is in flashback leading up to the violation, the second what happens subsequently: the death of the perpetrator when he is pushed out of his third-floor window by the victim and her friend. He 'falls' from one side of the stage onto the other.

Hit 'em hard at the beginning and at the end!

It was due to be performed over three nights, Thursday through to Saturday, though by the Thursday morning bookings were disappointing and opening on Saturday seemed touch-and-go.

Although I wanted to ask questions about right and wrong, judgement and punishment etcetera, I had no idea how the audience would receive it. That's part of the drama of writing — or the drama of drama — you have no control over how an audience will respond. You write what you write and send it out to fend for itself. After that… It's a thrill and a privilege — which is something I can afford to say given, well, that I can now afford to say it.

Apart from being a bit rough in places, Thursday was a triumph. The murmurings from the audience when they left were in a low register, intense. And word got out. Friday's bookings really picked up. Saturday we were full.

"A Minor Masterpiece" said the local rag on the Monday.

- You didn't like the word 'minor'.

- But the other two words were okay…

- And how did you feel about exposing our mother in such a way?

- It isn't her story.

- It's the story of all women.

Matty was entitled to his opinion. But I shut him up for a while, just in case.

~

JAYNE and CORAL are sitting in deckchairs on their side of the stage looking out toward the audience. There is a period of silence. We get the sense of a pause in a difficult conversation.

CORAL   So, are you going to the police?

JAYNE   [*shakes her head*] What are they going to do? This is Brighton in the summer. They're probably inundated with claims of wrongdoing, men against young women.

CORAL   Even so.

JAYNE   His word against mine; that's all it will be.

CORAL   But what about the evidence?

JAYNE   What evidence? It's not the kind of thing that leaves you with visible scars. Bruises maybe — but you could just as easily have got those by bumping into the fridge or tripping over a carpet.

CORAL   [*pause; thinking*] What about the binoculars?

JAYNE   Telescope.

CORAL   Telescope then.

JAYNE   Maybe he's not stupid. Maybe he keeps it pointed at the sky most of the time. "I'm an amateur astrologist"; that's all he needs to say. Have a few books lying around. Or he could chuck it in the cupboard for a while.

CORAL   He won't do that?

JAYNE   Why not?

CORAL   Perverts like that are usually addicted aren't they? He'll be scouring the beach every day. Maybe even now. And maybe he'll be looking for you.

JAYNE shivers involuntarily. They continue to look out to the audience. Silence. JAYNE turns to look to the other half of the stage, as if she is trying to locate the flat where the assault took place.

On the other side of the stage, a spotlight picks out CLYNE as he peers at JAYNE and CORAL through his telescope.

CORAL   So. What <u>are</u> you going to do? You can't do nothing.

JAYNE   What you said about him looking. I think I've had an idea — but I'm going to need your help.

CORAL   Why don't I like the sound of that?

JAYNE   It's only a little play-acting — and after all, you're the one who's keen for me to do something.

~

That was something of a theme for me back then, the wanting to tackle difficult subjects. I've heard people refer to the period as a 'rite of passage' — whatever the hell one of those is! Isn't every piece, every day, every word, a rite of passage? From my perspective, I was interested in pushing the boundaries — of both subject and form — to see what I could achieve.

No. That's incorrect.

First and foremost I wanted to find out where the boundaries were. Or if there were any at all; and if so, how they were imposed. Externally? Internally based on the limitations of language? Or derived, consciously or unconsciously, by me based on either talent or some moral failsafe? Individual members of the audience would come armed with their own red lines.

Ensconced with Hazel soon after *Sunbathing*'s success (perhaps the play helped me win her over, which would be ironic, wouldn't it?) I started dabbling in fiction again; short stories mainly. Having had two hits out of two (or three, if you must include *Frigid Air*), whether I thought I'd cracked playwriting I've no idea. The 'me' I now am doubts it — but I wouldn't be surprised if that's how the 'me' then saw it.

You're spending so much of your time writing these days. And if I was, then it would have been on those exploratory little stories; vignettes more than anything else. 'Sharpening my pencil' is how I once described it to an interviewer.

- Pompous arse!

- For once I'm not going to disagree.

Later — when was it, about seven years ago? — they took the trouble to persuade me to resurrect those yarns, collect them together, add a title. Well, at the time it was easy money for all of us...

But there was nothing in them as raw as *Sunbathing*, not in terms of subject matter. If being with Hazel had enabled me to get into a better writing rhythm, then it also narrowed my range. Oh, I still tried to find the edges of things, but somehow all within the context of my relationship with her. Redefined boundaries. It was as if she'd applied a firebreak between me and what I was really interested in.

- And after?

- After we split up, you mean?

- After she left you.

I don't know. Or I do know.

I woke up one morning to find that the firebreak had vanished with her. I sat down and started writing something new, and I found I could push my words through where the false boundary had been, the one she had constructed without me even realising it. Or the one 'love' had constructed.

If you're minded to do so you can look at it like that: love become the 'bad guy', the cowboy in the black hat, the scheming woman in *Dangerous Liaisons*.

Not wanting to risk being constrained by another firebreak would certainly have given me an additional excuse as to why I never subsequently sought 'love': for all it might give me, what became more significant was the fear as to what it could take away. Or prevent me from discovering. Maybe that's what I realised, or how I justified myself.

Avalanche was a metaphor, of course: a man on a skiing holiday, separated from his friends, goes off-piste and gets caught in a minor avalanche. Finds himself buried in snow. And while he awaits rescue (because he's convinced he will be rescued) he contemplates the nature of being alone, of being subjugated to uncontrollable external forces; he weighs up the recent events in his life which, yes, happens to include a broken relationship! By the time he is found and dug out (still just about clinging to life), he has reassessed himself and his priorities, discovered a new coda.

- And that was you?

Truthfully, I was scared about writing it. I mean, I had the idea and I liked it, but I had no clue where it would take me.

Nor if I might be changed come the end of it — though we're changed by everything we write, aren't we? I suppose I wrote it because in one sense I'd chosen to bury myself.

- Because you wanted to be rescued?

- No. Because I wanted to be buried!

Not that it was about Hazel. Not really. In fact, I don't think I've ever written about her, not the tangible person, how we were. Slivers here and there transposed into and onto unreal characters, but nothing more. Not until now. Until this — which remember is not a memoir.

Rather it's another boundary to be crossed.

- The final firebreak?

- If you like.

~

Everything is grey. You expect it to be white because snow is white. Blindingly so. Dangerously so. Sunglasses and visors. But when you're surrounded by it, *absorbed* in it, unable to see the sky until you work out which way is up, until you try to punch a hole through the canopy, then snow is grubby, dirty. Not pure and driven at all, but filled with debris — perhaps the result of the avalanche and what came down with it: bits of twig, leaf, fragments of rock from how much further up the mountain? It's like being cocooned in a microcosm of history.

Not that I have been able to punch through and release the sky. Not yet. I am too tired. More significantly, my right shoulder hurts so much that I can't use that arm to apply force to anything. I have scraped at a little of the snow immediately surrounding me, and with my left hand managed to force my broken ski pole upwards (the pole, broken like my life) hoping it will have compromised the surface like a submarine's periscope. Cramped as I am, I will jiggle it again in a few minutes, try to enlarge the aperture, to see the sky. Did you know that first and foremost periscopes were used to supply air to submariners?

85

Snow is heavy and grey. And it's unexpectedly warm too. Almost cosy. It would be easy to snuggle down and doze off. Easy but fatal. So I must keep my wits about me, invest in a routine to work away with the pole, and give myself something to occupy my mind.

Which, of course, can only be you. Fitting, don't you think, given the unreliable nature of snow?

~

But it's an interesting question, isn't it, how far one is prepared to go in that constant searching? As writers, I mean. Unless you're one of those non-original types who sticks to a formula: 'cosy crime' perhaps, or Mills & Boon. Though I've never understood such people. Why be satisfied with the second-rate — unless you've no choice of course, or don't have the wherewithal to make your own mark. In the shadow of giants rather than on their shoulders.

Not that I'm claiming…

But there *has* to be a point, doesn't there? And if I've a reputation for tackling the uncomfortable from time to time, well, I suppose that's deserved. Because I have. The human side of war, of rape, what it means to be alone — even some cockamamy stream of consciousness academic essay!

Although you may think it unnecessarily confrontational, I like to believe I have a "so what?" approach. After I've read something I often ask "so what?": what difference has that writing made to me, to you, the world? Is it trying to say something important? And if not, then what was the point of it? I have never wanted to risk putting myself in the situation where some obnoxious sod can ask *those* questions of *my* writing; someone who, in the face of my complicit silence, comes up with the wrong answer.

I wanted everything I produced to matter — even *Frigid Air.* Is that such a crime?

Making things matter has always been a motivation. And where best to find the most difficult and challenging subjects than in the realm of taboo? Not simply war or being alone, but rape too. Then religion, violence. And sex, of course — though people always made far too much of that. I never saw it as 'a focus area'; I was simply examining one of the core elements of being human. Perhaps some people found my treatment of women coarse or degrading, but then perhaps they were also folk who found any kind of flesh troublesome, always ready to draw parallels between my writing, my life, and depravity — just to protect themselves. Mine was a sex life largely without love remember, so I could allow the writing of it to be raw even if there were a few women, temporarily attached to me, who tried to paint our shared episodes in a softer hue.

~

Painted in the Dark Corner took those who thought I was developing a one-track mind by surprise. That might have been most people, I guess. It did so partly because there wasn't any obvious sex in it (though there was a glimmer if you looked hard enough!), and partly because it was a story about mental illness, a nervous breakdown, the debilitation caused by a collapsed mind.

"Where did that come from?" many asked. I can remember the shock in some of the reviews. And the plaudits.

The answer to the question is obvious, isn't it? It came from me. How could it not? And if people assumed I'd done my research, spent time in 'institutions', then I wasn't going to disabuse them. That added to the frisson, gave the narrative an extra degree of credibility. In a way it made me more interesting. But the only institution in which I'd spent time was my own head; the only breakdown I knew anything about was my own — that is if you don't count what happened to Valerie near the end, after Jack died.

- And do you?

- Do I what?

- Count that.

- It depends where I'm looking at it from. Doesn't everything? Isn't context and perspective the dominant influence always? Valerie wasn't relevant when it came to *Dark Corner;* I was. Simple as. If you'd been paying attention all these years you'd understand that.

- I've been too busy not being here.

- As if.

What do I remember most about it — not *Dark Corner* itself, but what led up to it? The fear mostly. And don't forget, I'd only just turned thirty. Wasn't I too young for such an experience?

I can tell you exactly how it started: me sitting on the edge of the bed unable to move. I was due to go to work, nothing other than that; an ordinary day. Yes, work was becoming a little difficult; boring and uninspiring. Increasingly I'd begun to resent that I needed to give up my time in order to feed myself. I had three public triumphs to my name (okay, *small* public triumphs), a number of other pieces, the beginnings of a reputation. Maybe I thought that should be enough.

The previous day I'd finished with a girl who had started to become a little too intense. It had been a painful day. Maybe there were echoes of Hazel kicking around. Or of others too. I don't really recall.

Probably others.

I'd swung my legs out of bed and was just about to get up, to walk to the bathroom, go through the motions, when I found I couldn't move. It was a kind of paralysis. It *was* paralysis. My head was both empty *and* swimming, as if I had managed to bring my recent life, every individual granule of it, to the forefront and now all those components were jostling for priority, demanding attention. And each and every one was asking questions: why this, why that. Voices; a cacophony of voices. And I had no idea which to listen to… If Matty was also in there somewhere I didn't hear him.

Yet strangely, in spite of all that noise, that inner drama, the world was still and quiet. It was just me sitting on the edge of the bed. Life outside seemed to have been put on pause. I heard nothing; no birds, no road noise.

I've had people who think they're cleverer than me try to analyse that episode, those who believe they understood what was going on. But if *I* didn't, how could *they*? 'An existential crisis' was the most popular theory. You know, akin to asking "what's the point?"; not why am I here exactly, but what difference does me being here make? There might have been a whole compendium of complex esoteric questions bubbling away in the background, but there was just one on which I needed to focus: "Did I want to get up and go to work?"

I sat there for twenty minutes unable to answer it. Twenty minutes. It felt like a lifetime. The bedroom door kept zooming away from me and then back again like a Hitchcock dolly-shot. And in those twenty minutes I felt a new kind of fear: it was the fear of not being invincible; the fear of failure, of being worthless; the fear — if not the *certainty* — that my writing was no good; that I was inadequate, both as a writer and as a man; that my life was filled with mistakes and bad decisions.

Yet simultaneously — and in spite of the tumult — all remained quiet and still.

Eventually I managed to haul myself up and go to the bathroom. I had a shit and a shower. I phoned-in sick, then took myself off into town, walked the arboretum, sat in coffee shops. It was almost a reorientation, an attempt to re-familiarise myself with 'normal' as if in doing so I might find my place in the world again.

Can you imagine what that's like, to suddenly find yourself comprehensively and profoundly lost? Only if you've had a similar experience, I suggest. I look at my description of those terrifying few minutes and know I have only scratched the surface. Me, with my arsenal of words, my invention, my years of experience — and now one of the 'old men' of English literature, if you believe what you read on the dust covers of books…

~

There is a chasm between me and the bathroom door. A chasm of two metres. I look down to my feet expecting to see them welded to the carpet, their fixing executed surreptitiously the instant they hit the floor. As if the floor is varnished with a layer of glue so powerful… And now the adhesive has risen to the bed, fixes me there by the seat of my pyjamas, my hands at my side resting on the mattress. I fear speaking, as if doing so will allow the resin to infest my mouth, freeze my jaw in mid-scream. I turn my head. The clock on the bedside table ticks remorselessly, its second-hand taunting me with its movement, the counting on — or counting down — somehow doom-laden, measuring out the extent of my paralysis.

Five minutes. Or six.

Through the partially open en-suite door I see a sliver of the shower screen, half of the sink; and I imagine the toilet around the corner. In my mind I try and project myself there — on the toilet, in the shower, brushing my teeth at the basin — hoping that will act as an antidote to the glue, a solvent to release me from where I sit.

But I do not move.

Seven minutes.

Outside the bedroom door, just two paces would take me to the top of the stairs; then down thirteen steps into the hall, through to the kitchen to fill up the kettle, prepare a small coffee, a bowl of cereal... But these actions, still ephemeral, are no solvent either; and unlike the bathroom, they pose additional questions, apply another layer of fixative to my immobility. "Why?" they ask. Why make the coffee, indulge in breakfast; for what reason to then reascend the stairs, finish dressing, make my way back down, collect my keys, lock the house, walk into town? Locking and unlocking seemed such redundant activities — especially when remaining fixed, statue-like, is the only option.

Eight minutes now.

And so I search for difference, variation that comes with doing and not-doing. I try and sift through the rubble of my thoughts to find a nugget of truth — like a miner panning for gold. But all I can see is rubble, fragments of rock, valueless pyrite. Closing my eyes, I try to let my ears re-locate me, establish the 'where' and 'when' and 'how' of me via noises from the road outside, the birds in the garden. But I hear nothing. It is as if the glue has now infested my ears.

I am paralysed, mute, and deaf.

Nine minutes.

~

Don't ask me how long it took to fully come round from the subsequent malaise because I can't tell you. In an odd way it was a little like starting a new journey, a fresh quest. Just standing up from the bed was setting sail knowing I had to find my way home — *and* travel through hostile territory to do so. Odysseus all over again.

When did I find a truly safe harbour? Again, no idea.

A couple of days later I was back into my routine, though somehow in a much more low-key and tentative way. Maybe I didn't write anything for a few days, a couple of weeks, a month... If you pushed me, I suppose I could search out some evidence in order to be precise. Though that's hardly relevant.

What *is* more relevant (and on reflection, satisfyingly inevitable) was that I *did* start writing again — and in doing so was compelled to try and deconstruct that awful experience; to decode it, pick it apart, first to component level and then beyond that, down to its very atoms. Should it have been surprising that when I'd decided to do so, I found myself in front of a blank new document on my computer screen unable to move my fingers? For how long? Twenty minutes again? I don't know; it could have been. Art imitating life and all that. But I suspect it only seemed like an age.

I was faced with a different kind of fear, of course. Not the usual mix of anxiety and excitement you get when you start to work on something new, when you're mesmerised in a positive way, but rather something deeper, more raw. Maybe that was because I had no idea what I would find, nor what that finding would do to me.

If you looked at my work through the lens of personal entanglement, everything I'd written to that point was really tangental: *Tainted Harvest* was historical theory; *Frigid Air* was almost an 'anti-me'; in *Sunbathing* I was neither the rapist nor the person raped, but rather a different kind of voyeur. I don't think I was even Valerie's son. Maybe I'd concede *Avalanche*, just a little. But *Dark Corner* was different. There was no way I could remove myself from the story I was trying to narrate there. I needed to lay down words culled from personal experience, as if I was somehow peeling back *my* skin, each word representing another few cells, a persistent exposing of what lay beneath. And it was scary in that I found I could go as deep as I wanted. Or as I needed to.

When I was half-way through drafting, it dawned on me that the story would need a conclusion, a conclusion I had yet to experience. I almost stopped writing it there and then. Given I'd not yet fully processed the event myself, how could I possibly know how it ended? Or then again, I wondered if in some way the writing *was* the ending, and if so what did that imply? That notion may have been nothing more than me trying to con myself out of a difficult situation; yet it also struck me that might be where the real discovery lay, in my fabricating an ending, both to the fictional story and the real event itself. Almost in parallel. And if what I wrote was somehow prescient? What if in the story — and perhaps in mortal fear of its conclusion, who knows? — I was doing nothing more than trying to postpone an inevitable tragedy? Or was predicting one?

It proved difficult for me to convince myself that the narrative was a fiction; that at a fundamental level it was divorced from me and my reality; that no matter how the main character's life might mirror my own, in the end it was all his and none of it was mine. And even if he ended up sitting on the edge of the bed for twenty minutes, *he* would be doing that, not me; and it would be on *his* fictitious bed and not my real one.

And if he jumped from a high building…?

There was some comfort in persuading myself of the existence of that gap (firebreaks again!), the undeniable divide between fiction and reality, between him and me.

But later — either subconsciously soon after I wrote *Dark Corner*, or consciously and much more recently, who can say? — I began to see *my* existence as being as much of a fiction as my *Dark Corner* character's. Indeed, as all my characters. Perhaps *I* might have been the greatest fabrication of all. In its way this was another pivot point on the journey, another ending or another beginning.

Was acknowledgement of that divide between fiction and reality the ultimate conclusion, the most significant and binary realisation of a thirty-year-old man who had experienced what it was like to sit on the edge of a bed unable to move? Both the source event and my analysis of it may have been like staring into the abyss. Others have suggested as much.

Protected by forty-seven years of forgetfulness, of selective amnesia, I have no final theory. Nor do I want one. Not really. A younger version of myself was on the verge of some kind of breakdown — and managed to haul himself out of it. He had stared something awful in the face and been shit-scared. Fear had been redefined for him.

And the struggle? Eventually the battle was fought out on the page, in the spaces between commas and full stops, between pages one and two, then two and three. It wasn't the whole war, of course. It doesn't bear thinking about it being the whole war — especially had it been a war I'd lost. But it was a battle nonetheless, and it needed fighting, not hiding from. And where would I have hidden anyway? So I armed myself with paper and ink, software and keyboard, and I took on fear and uncertainty; I deployed the only troops I could muster and deployed them on the field of battle — the virgin white of the screen, the page — and awaited the outcome.

~

Everyone knows. As I walk from the car park towards the mall I sense people looking my way — but when I scan their faces, try to catch them staring, they all manage to be looking elsewhere, pretending to be absorbed by the trial of the stairs, the waiting for the lift, the raucous children careening ahead of them. And the mall is full of them too, these prying, knowing faces, each of them camouflaged in the admiration of window displays, or heading into the perfumed and air-conditioned certainty of *Next* or *M&S*. But they know — and I know they know.

I take a seat in the window of my favourite café and look out, trying to catch them betraying themselves. My location is less an attempt to hide and more a statement of defiance. I *want* them to see; I *want* them to acknowledge my triumph in simply being here, the bravery which had eventually managed to lift me from the bed after twenty minutes and stumble slowly to the bathroom.

My macchiato arrives, borne by a waitress I recognise; yet there is something in her manner — the way she speaks, the slight shake of her hand as she deposits the coffee on the bench in front of me — which betrays her too, what she knows. Having left me, I imagine her back at the counter talking to her colleagues, pointing subtly in my direction — "see that guy over there…" — and not only do her colleagues look at me but everyone else in the café does too. It is as if I have a sign pinned to my back which says 'this man could not get out of bed'. Or 'victim of paralysis'. Or some such negatively-loaded phrase. And as I look up from the coffee, out into the mall where the passers-by also fail to look my way, I am certain I am being judged — and found wanting.

~

Sometimes when you survive something I think you end up diminished, not strengthened as common legend would have it: "what hurts you makes you stronger", or some such. You can be depleted by the effort or denuded by the process. And me at the beginning of the 80s? Drained rather than depleted, I suppose. But also soon to be re-energised by survival; buoyed by my ability to get back up, to tell the story. And probably hoping to be free once again, this time having secured a new lens through which to examine my life: Charles E. the detached narrator, story-teller, translator, voyager. But also Charles E. as a fiction: his life — and the lives of all those he touched — reimagined as a 'confection' to be dissected between the covers of a book; replayed, massaged and manipulated, redacted and embellished; presented in little packages of foil or twisted paper. 'Confection'; 'con-fiction'…

- Was that where I came in?

- Came in? No, not really. You'd been there all along. But you were different after that.

- As were you.

- I meant in our relationship.

- Whereas I did not…

Was my conclusion — Charles E., a character of my own making — too fanciful or too neat? Was it a 'get out of jail card' and a license to do, well, anything I wanted?

Excrement

1981 - 1984

Anything I wanted including, as it turned out, drafting shit.

Even though *Painted in a Dark Corner* wasn't published until much later, finishing it made me more confident than ever, more certain of where I was heading. If I could handle such a difficult — and personal — subject, surely nothing would now be out-of-bounds. It was that old immortality returning.

Not only did my survival of the crisis — *and* the story it inspired — feed this sensation, so did the burgeoning notion of creating a second Charles E., one who was a work of fiction. I was beginning to become my own plaything, a character to be exploited, manipulated. In order to prove a point — and, I suppose, to put even more distance between myself and Hazel — I allowed the embryonic 'unreal' me to embark on two ruthlessly quick affairs: one with a slightly older woman who also happened to work in Boots (Hazel had left the store by then), and another who waitressed in a small restaurant up in Bailgate. They were empty encounters (at least on my side) designed to do no more than demonstrate that I was still attractive — and to further shape the new persona I was crafting for my 'fictional' thirty-two year-old self.

Although I've never much cared for Michael Caine, when I was seventeen I had — like many young men — been fascinated by *Alfie,* and now found myself in a position to enact a surrogate version of his life. A little slice of the East End in Lincolnshire. Apart from enjoying the vacuous and hedonistic sex, from a writerly perspective I was not only interested in cultivating material for future projects but also keen to explore how my doppelgänger might break through the 'forth wall'. It was as if — like Alfie — I could see myself as the lead actor in my own drama.

- Not that you hadn't already tried that.

- You think I had?

- Just listen to yourself.

Those two brief encounters were no more than elongated one-night-stands, experiments in self-definition. And I never pretended they were anything other than that. I tell myself the two women concerned went into them — both the dalliances and my arms — with their eyes open. At least most of the time! All these years later they remain what they always were: the inconsequential exploits of a youngish man trying to re-find his feet — and a writer trying to recapture his mojo.

If you wanted to be prudish about it, I'll admit it was not my finest hour — nor is my inability to remember the girls' names (though whether you believe me about that or not is up to you). They were affairs which weren't intended to be anything other than the infusion of colour in a new fictional character — even if that character was essentially me. And importantly, maybe they also acted as kindling for what would I would try a few years later.

~

Was it unrealistic of me to expect big things from my first novel? I think I'd labelled it as 'my breakthrough' even before I'd finished it; in fact even before I'd landed an agent. I used a rough draft of the first ten thousand words and an over-inflated track-record to blag my way into the mainstream.

Although officially based in the West End, Declan Peel spent a fair chunk of his time working out of a small office in Nottingham. Being able to get to Nottingham on the train was one of the reasons I sounded him out. He must have been about forty-eight when I met him, and although contracted to Macmillan, he occasionally moonlighted for some smaller operators. When I walked him through my idea for *Beyond Dominance* Declan wasn't that impressed.

It was a story about a forty-year-old man who, having been cheated on by his wife, decides to embrace his new-found sexual freedom — but ends up facing into the consequences of his miscalculation. In hindsight I can't blame Declan for his caution. Initially it was a crude *Alfie* / *Basic Instinct* / *Fifty Shades of Grey* mash-up, even if we were many years before *Fifty Shades* was ever an idea. *It sounds*, he said, *like cliché and derivative fantasy fulfilment.* I was reminded of Horberry — which was enough for me to persist. Declan offered a concession. *In the end, whether I touch it or not will depend on how well it's written.*

There was just about enough in what I'd already achieved for him to take me seriously, and the plot for *Dominance* clearly interested him — though on what level I was never entirely sure. Although he especially liked the Greek Tragedy denouement, I think the clincher proved to be that he admired *Avalanche,* a draft of which I'd sent him as part of my 'portfolio'. He said he'd see if he could get *Avalanche* placed somewhere significant: *That may be the Litmus Test.*

Luckily he knew Bill Buford, the first editor of the relaunched *Granta*, and decided to try it out with him. A Litmus Test of the highest order! When Bill took my story, Declan agreed to represent me and take on *Dominance*. He made suggestions about plot and so forth. I listened; adopted some of his ideas, rejected most.

I may have been reinventing myself, but hadn't yet recognised — nor therefore eliminated — the fact that I was still a bit of a prick!

I probably started drafting the final version of *Dominance* around September '81. In order to devote myself to it — and, finally, to my *real* career! — I reduced the amount of paid work I was doing thus freeing up more time to write. Consequently, life became increasingly spartan. Perhaps I was just living another cliché, fulfilling an image of what I thought a writer was supposed to be: impoverished and garret-bound.

If I didn't recognise some of the implications of my new lifestyle — nor that in parallel I was continuing to develop and partition the fictional 'me' — I also didn't see what *Beyond Dominance* was really about. I thought, *Alfie*-like, it concerned a man getting his comeuppance; a story of manipulation which came at a price — one eventually paid by all those concerned. I think I'd had this vague notion that, because in the end the guy gets mortally undone by one of the women he's been mistreating, it was enlightened; 'a woman's novel'. But it wasn't of course; it was too coarse for that. *Dominance* was all about anger: the anger I still felt at Hazel's betrayal and which I hadn't finished processing; plus the anger I felt towards myself for being weak. I hadn't been strong enough — or wise enough — to keep her; I hadn't been strong enough to stop turning myself into some sad wreckage who couldn't get out of bed; and I hadn't been strong enough to be honest with both myself and the women who came both before and after her.

Of course, none of that stopped me from having a draft to deliver to Declan by the end of the year.

The writing shows promise, he said when we met mid-January in Nottingham. *Real promise. But let's face it Charles, the story's still a bit shitty.* Would it be shitty today? I doubt it.

Heading back to Lincoln, I sat on the train wondering if Declan wasn't merely Horberry mark-II. There was a part of me that already wanted to dispose of him, to denigrate his opinion — after all, "the story's shitty" was as damning as it came. But if he knew Bill Burford then he knew other people too. *And* he'd got *Avalanche* into *Granta*; *and* he had a decent track record, representing one or two 'names' at Macmillan.

When the train reached Newark Castle I watched a young couple get on. The man, probably late thirties, was clearly in the early stages of some debilitating disease (which I would later assume was Parkinson's); the woman helping him was a few years younger. Not many. Initially I wondered if she might be a nurse or a carer come to take him to Lincoln for a break; or perhaps he had an appointment at the hospital. Then I noticed their wedding rings, the way she spoke to him, that undefinable something in the way she held his arm, his elbow.

I've had people describe that train journey from Nottingham to Lincoln as an epiphany — which, of course, is bollocks. But it *was* something…

In an interview (not that long ago, actually) someone suggested that, as far as the train scene was concerned, the ailing man represented me and the woman Declan, the metaphor being the notion of the helping hand, assistance in making the journey. Clearly crap! Others — those in the 'epiphany' camp — suggested the vignette showed me how relationships between men and women *could* be, that they needn't be driven or defined by the carnal.

Nowadays I can't be bothered to argue. It hardly matters. The person I was on the train that day is no more than a ghost. Probably less than a ghost, given I'm haunting no-one other than myself.

- And doing a pretty good job of it I'd say.

- If I need your opinion, I'll ask for it…

At some point between Newark and Lincoln I became resolved: Declan was right. My new novel *was* shit. But not — and this was important — unredeemable; there were elements in its basic framework that were sound. And Declan hadn't told me to throw it away, just as he hadn't said our relationship was over. *I'll still be on your team*, he said, *but only if you think carefully about reshaping the story.*

Was that the clincher: the fact he hadn't dismissed me, hadn't said my draft was beyond saving? Or was it because I liked him?

I wasn't known for liking people I couldn't sleep with.

Completely unpicking something I'd written and then knitting it back together wasn't a skill I'd practiced much. You don't, do you? In the early days everything you write is so bloody perfect that you don't need to. Even when it isn't! As it turned out, Declan hadn't 'taught' me anything — not in the strictest sense of the word — but he *had* superimposed a new view on the imperative; he gave me a better sense of what needed to be done. Thinking *Beyond Dominance* was all done and dusted, I'd left Lincoln to meet him with no notion other than it was finished — but returned a few hours later with its incompleteness uppermost in my mind.

The knack, I now know, is process. It's always process. The question — surfaced by an entirely new challenge — was how to take something I'd produced and then reconstruct it in as detached a manner as possible, coldly, as if I hadn't even written it. No-one tells you how to do that. They tell you how to hone your craft, improve your skills; they give you tips about putting words together — but they don't tell you how to take them apart.

My first instinct was to look at *Dominance* on the screen, pretty much as a reader might. Nothing happened. The words seemed coherent enough. After a couple of hours all I had done was to play with punctuation, swapped one or two sentences about. Tinkering. And I knew it needed more than tinkering. So I tried a different tack. I asked myself "do I *need* this chapter?"; then if 'yes', "do I *need* this paragraph?"; then again if 'yes', "do I *need* this sentence?" — you get the picture. In a new version of the document, I had the computer put a line through anything I didn't think had earned its place: two whole chapters, about ten percent of the paragraphs, and twenty percent of the sentences. In the end I'd turned an able-bodied novel into a skeleton — probably with a couple of ribs missing! Or worse than that: just a pile of bones lying on the metaphorical desk where I worked.

That's a much better metaphor!

After that I reassembled, swapped some things around; discovered where bones were missing and — stretching the metaphor — found where I needed to attach fresh ligaments, reconstitute muscles. Frankenstein-like, I rebuilt the novel from most of its original components but now also included bits I'd scavenged from elsewhere or had to create from scratch.

It took another two-and-a-half months. It was a time when I became a monk, a social outcast; I drank little, hardly went out. Apart from one brief encounter with an old flame (which I chose to regard as 'research'!) I remained celibate. I thought about Hazel and betrayal, and remoulded my characters a little, drafting new skins on one or two. In the end it would have been easy to regard it as a different book — but one retaining the original title.

If I felt drained by the time I made my return to Nottingham with draft mark-II it was hardly surprising. I'd cleaned out the stables and in the process arrived at a new and strenuous methodology, one which required me to change the modus operandi of the writer I was. I'd embraced the need to live reclusively, to write as ruthlessly and objectively as I could. Yet sometimes it was still a struggle to maintain an emotional equilibrium; more than once I'd wanted to throw the fucking thing away and start again. Or stop writing entirely.

Perhaps that applied to both the book *and* the new life it was forcing me into.

Where did that come from?! Declan asked when I rang him a week after handing my new baby over. I didn't really have an answer for him. *The bottom of the barrel* had been my only suggestion. *It's sparse, lean, taut; filled with energy and menace. It doesn't pull any punches. It's modern, decisive, radical.* I had no idea what he meant about 'decisive' and 'radical' but I didn't push it; he was enthusiastic, that's what counted.

Another pivot point. Another beginning.

~

"I don't know how you manage to do what you do."

"What do you mean?"

As he considered Caleb, he couldn't help but mark the lines on a face which hadn't been there three years earlier, the trace of grey in the hair about his temple. Yes, his new glasses still managed to convey something of his old boyish charm, but this was merely the application of a cosmetic; Harry knew his friend was changed. Beyond recognition? Not quite — but surely that day was not far off.

"Looking after Alice the way you do."

Caleb laughed, but it was a laugh without humour.

"If I don't, who does?"

Harry had always assumed that was what the State was there for, to help people in need — both the sick and those who were impacted by that sickness. Providing such support was why he voted, paid his taxes. Freedom — at least freedom as he defined it — was worth paying for. He shrugged his shoulders.

Caleb continued.

"Not that I'd expect you to understand; 'in sickness and in health' and all that. Hardly your area of expertise."

"'Til death us do part'?"

"If you like." Caleb's tone was flat. It was the tone of a man caught in a trap; the kind of trap Harry had vowed he would never fall into.

"Maybe it's just a matter of time," Harry suggested. "Maybe I haven't met the right girl yet."

Another laugh from Caleb, this time laced with a combination of bitterness, incredulity, a hint of sadness. Harry could forgive him the laugh because of the latter.

"What?"

"You've probably already met 'the right girl'. Maybe more than one — or certainly a few who would fit the bill. But you either weren't looking straight or you're after some kind of paragon who simply doesn't exist."

It was the kind of complaint he often heard from his mother; after all, how was he going to satisfy her desire for grandchildren if he didn't 'settle down'?

"You might be right," Harry agreed, an emptiness in his voice. It was a hollow and disingenuous concession because he profoundly disagreed with his friend. He hadn't found his equivalent to Alice because he wasn't looking for 'the right girl' at all. Often any girl was right enough.

~

And how do I feel about it now, after so many more beginnings and endings, both real and fake?

I don't really know.

But then I've written that with the air of a man who absolutely *does* know. I hope you picked that up! The *Beyond Dominance* period was an episode which taught me about the importance of detachment and analysis, about being ruthless. Here was a discovery that words weren't sacrosanct after all, not in and of themselves. They were handmaidens, transports to pleasure and communication which needed to be massaged and manipulated — and then fearlessly cast aside if they failed in their task. More echoes of *Alfie*, perhaps?

Throwing words away. That was an important lesson.

And I learned about myself too. Not merely the fact that I could devote myself to a task — 'suffer for my art' (if you want to see it that way) — but that I was prepared to listen. First to Declan, obviously (how fundamental was *but let's face it, the story's shitty?*), but also to myself; not the conscious me, the one geeing myself up, spurring me on, but the one who existed in the ether, the product of my history and its vast cast; all those prior versions of me; all my past lives with each one reincarnated, every person I'd ever encountered a teacher.

- Even me?

- Perhaps especially you; who knows?

That's all very inflated though, isn't it? The notion of the 'whole self' or however you might want to label it. But as I tried to create this fictional version of myself — perhaps *especially* because I was trying to do so — I discovered I was still in danger of falling for the delusion that I was 'enough'; that all I needed to *be* me *was* me. Self-sufficiency run amok. *Dominance* helped me understand that one version of me wasn't enough. Declan's *the story's shitty* had been the trigger, the invasion from outside my writing needed. Maybe that my life needed.

Oh, I know you're going to ask *what about Hazel?* — but she's a different matter entirely. Not from the perspective of my writing, but because my experience with her is obviously included in the compendium, emotionally... The two — my life, and my life with Hazel — are discrete. I discovered that too. Not that one's a subset of the other, nor subservient to it, but rather that they're entwined, overlapping. Like a Venn diagram. And every new beginning, every new encounter, every new project, wasn't a start from scratch but the overlay of a fresh circle on an increasingly complex diagram and evidenced by a blank page with "Chapter" written at the top of it.

My life as a fiction, even there.

- And do you believe that?

- Believe what?

- All that nonsense about learning and beginnings and fictions.

- Is there a reason I shouldn't?

- Interesting.

- What is?

- That you didn't respond to my question with the certainty of 'yes', or to tell me to 'fuck off' like you usually do — especially when I express an opinion.

- I don't do that.

- Okay; so it must be the fictional 'you' who does. Sorry Bro.

Ignore him.

And underpinning that new experience — or if not underpinning it, somehow interwoven with it — was my beginning to understand the role history plays in pulling together the future. Or the 'now'. We drag our history kicking and screaming into the present — *and* simultaneously burden ourselves with it. We're always doused in the after-birth of our past. Always. As we get older the volume of that sticky mucus only increases, and opportunities to cleanse ourselves of it reduce. We're held back by it. We're not in thrall — that would be too positive — but rather trapped. Trapped by our history.

Not that's how I saw it then of course. *Beyond Dominance* was evidence of learning, a new beginning, something different, and not another nail in the coffin — even if everything, everywhere and always, is another nail in the coffin.

- Just like this?

- This? This *is* the fucking coffin.

But it hadn't been then. Declan was right; *Dominance* was all those things he said it was, and perhaps more. He landed a good deal with a publisher (not much of an advance, but a decent royalty) and then worked his arse off it get it into bookshops, libraries, and onto bookclub reading lists.

The cover helped. It was dark and menacing, suggesting a racy horror-thriller hybrid all wrapped up in something conventional and contemporary. Which in a way it was. If you picked it off the shelf you'd be intrigued. God, *I* was intrigued and I'd written the bloody thing!

He told me not to expect too much. He was good like that. I think he knew we were on to something, but he didn't want to over-inflate. Self-protection on his part; after all, by then I'd already come to think of him as some kind of magic man, a miracle worker, someone who'd understood what I'd written — seen through me too, in a way — *and* been able to steer, shape, cajole… And then to be so commercially astute. If it was a hit, he wanted to ensure that, as best he could, he kept his hands on the reins. On my reins.

Five thousand copies; that would be a good outcome, he said. Five thousand was a decent level of sales for a first novel. It was proof of talent, might open doors to other things, other opportunities. If we were lucky we might get a few more.

~

What people fail to realise is that there's always a balance to be struck. A literary agent is constantly walking a tightrope: we have to be supportive, helpful and constructive when it comes to our clients, but at the same time mindful of what publishers are looking for, what will sell and therefore what we can pitch to them. You could say they're our clients too — and we're the jam squashed in the middle.

Charles was a robust enough character — and sufficiently self-confident — for me to be honest with him. If there was something I didn't like, I'd tell him. I know he's referred to what I said about the original incarnation of Beyond Dominance *more than once, and how that helped him make the book work. There are writers I couldn't possibly say such things to — but then I try to avoid the ones who are too delicate, where I feel I'm constantly on eggshells. If an author is fragile, most often their writing is fragile too.*

Having said that — and in spite of what Charles may have thought at the time, or said later — I still wasn't really convinced we'd have a success on our hands with **Beyond Dominance.** *I mean, you can never be certain. The book had a chance, but it was in the lap of the gods. In fact, it was a bit like readying a clay pot for firing and being at the mercy of the 'kiln gods'. Sometimes the final product is brilliant; sometimes it emerges shattered.*

That's the tightrope: "it's shitty" versus "it's brilliant". And most of the time neither are entirely true. Or entirely false.

Did we get lucky? Maybe. I was certainly fortunate I had a favour or two to call in; for sure that helped give the book some momentum. And momentum's everything. Throughout our association I tried to get Charles to realise that having 'a hit' wasn't enough; soon each and every triumph becomes devalued, yesterday's news. The only thing that mattered — if you were <u>really</u> going to make a go of your career — was the <u>next</u> effort, and then the one after that.

Oh, and what the publishers wanted from you. Increasingly that.

~

- And in the end?

- But you know the story.

- Yes, and I also know you like to tell it.

Sales started slowly, then it got a mention on a radio show. Prompted a few more. The big jump came when Frances Meredith popped up on daytime television and included it in her 'reads of the month'. I never found out how *that* happened, but I suspect either Declan knew her or money changed hands. Bookclubs became interested. Five thousand became fifteen thousand. *Beyond Dominance* made it to the edge of one of those promotional tables in Waterstones, WHSmith. It was 'commercial'.

In the end it sold over twenty thousand copies. I made a whole year's salary — maybe more — in just a few weeks.

How do you categorise that? Proof? Vindication? Luck? I'm sure what I felt back then — when the first royalty cheque arrived, when I had the first request for a newspaper interview — was entirely different to what I feel now.

- Which is?

- Is what? Now or then?

- Either. Or both. This is your story.

- Does it matter?

I would have been giddy, excited; probably filled with a sense of victory. Maybe I felt justified; that kind of "I told you so!" feeling. Which would have been perfectly natural, wouldn't it? I might have been a little unbearable too — if I'd had someone to be unbearable with, that is.

- And how do you see it now?

- Another step on the journey. Maybe no more than that. One that was logical, inevitable.

- Inevitable?

- Given what went before — and what I'd always believed. And, more especially, what came after. It had to start somewhere, didn't it? My career proper, that is.

Maybe such journeys are beginning all the time; always being energised, shaped, kick-started. Or failing. Those small steps.

The inevitability of that at least. It was another fragment in what instantly became my history, consigned to the past because it had been superseded by something else: a new 'now', another challenge, always a next step demanding to be taken. We can't stand still. Standing still is an impossibility. Motion is life. Or life is motion.

- But looking back from where you currently stand? Or maybe where you're standing still — in both senses of the phrase…

- I don't want to talk about 'now'. Not yet. I've not yet finished with 'then'.

It was a 'then' which allowed me to give up formal work. Abandoning work was the first thing I did the day after that cheque arrived: I paid it into the bank and resigned my old employee life. Walked out on it there and then. The action was instantaneous, imperative — and I didn't care how I made it happen, only that I did so.

Soon after that, I started to be invited to things: readings at bookshops, sitting on panels at events. Declan, consummate professional as he was then, engineered and handled all that. Not wanting to lean too heavily on the notion of *Beyond Dominance* being my first rodeo — and understanding the perils of me ending up being regarded as a one-hit-wonder — he made sure people were aware of what I'd done before: *Avalanche, Sunbathing*. Especially *Sunbathing*. Doing so added 'depth', he said; *it makes you more interesting, more complex. There will be more to talk about.* And he wasn't wrong.

I found myself moving in new circles, even if they were relatively small ones. It was a transition evidenced in practical ways: train journeys to London or Birmingham, Sheffield or Leeds; the need to adjust to a more fragmented domesticity, a new schedule, not merely of writing but also the humdrum; an increase in the volume of post I was getting. And out of the blue, the odd ex-girlfriend getting back in touch, my transgressions of the past forgiven. I suddenly had coat-tails some thought might be worth hanging on to.

- But not Hazel.

And I found myself wondering if I'd become a different person; whether the new me — or my embryonic fictional construct — had radically altered. Or even matured. Or was Charles mark-II taking over? How can you possibly hope to understand such things when you're immersed in them, soaked in the newness of the experience? Making it up as you go along, you juggle with such questions as best you can; only time and hindsight provide the true context, the most complete understanding…

If you pushed me, I would claim I was the same person I'd always been. But the fictional me..? Well, if anything, he was starting to achieve a greater definition I suppose. And a distinctiveness too.

But I was still only thirty-five. What the hell does anyone know at that age?

Birds

1985 - 1989

So what comes next?

This was the question Declan posed a few weeks later as we sat having a quiet pint, two anonymous blokes in a city centre pub early on a mid-week evening.

Next? I probably echoed, even if I totally understood what he wanted to know. His wasn't really a question anticipating a definitive answer; I think he just wanted to be comforted by knowing I was at least thinking about my next project. He had a view of course, and although he didn't immediately share it I would have been surprised had he endorsed the entirely conventional. Having found a seam, most writers mine it until it's exhausted, creating a series, a trilogy, the same theme or voice, the same character(s) spread thinly across multiple volumes. Even the same plot but with the scenery re-painted. Although he never explicitly said as much, he didn't want me to fall into the trap of working on some kind of sequel to *Beyond Dominance*.

Neither did I.

I told him about *Dark Corner* but said it wasn't really long enough for a novel. And in it's draft form it wasn't. Working it into something else was an option. *I'll think about it*, he said. *Maybe something for the future.*

I'd already arrived at a firm and unshakable notion that you didn't demonstrate the extent and depth of your talent by writing the same thing over and over. Maybe that showed wisdom, nous, or commercial naïvety. Or maybe arrogance, undue self-confidence. Not that I wasn't interested in displaying commercial awareness, of course I was; but the image I had of myself, that I'd been consciously forming and was now beginning to make real, was a portrait of someone who didn't repeat — at least not on the page. That was one of the beauties of giving birth to a fictional me: I could mould him in any way I saw fit.

Since *Tainted Harvest*, everything I'd written had — in some fundamental way or other — been different to what had come before. I told myself that doing so was essential to keep me interested, learning, on my toes. It kept my writing fresh. And it was a form of proof too. Maybe I can only push that argument now because of who I have become, with the evidence 'in the bank'; yet I can't help but wonder whether, aged thirty-five, I'd already formed an outline of how I wanted to be forty years further down the road and thus generated a schematic to which I needed to adhere. 'Fleshed out', if you like. Or filled-in, like a paint-by-numbers. If there was to be a journey, I may have already had a sense of my ultimate destination.

- This 'non-memoir'?

- Don't be an idiot, it doesn't become you.

- Nor you.

I've an idea, I told him; *something radical, a little more experimental*. He was, he said, 'intrigued'. After that I had to bat away his questions simply because at that stage (and two pints into a quiet four-pint evening) I'd nothing else to offer him.

My statement had nothing substantial behind it other than the knowing whatever came next would be different again.

From nowhere, a few weeks earlier, Frank had come to mind; and hot on Frank's heels, Professor Jensen and what he'd said about my *Ulysses* essay: *one of the most remarkable things I've ever seen*. From that remembrance, to ask myself "why not try something like that?" wasn't a huge leap to take. Jensen hadn't been passing comment on my academic prowess (not in *that* statement anyway!), but rather my embryonic mastery of craft, the ability to put one word in front of another in a creative way. Something beyond the norm. I'd thought about that essay on and off over the years and what it might 'mean'; maybe I always knew I'd come back to it, one way or another. At that precise moment, needing something new and wanting something different, why not take the style and structure of it for a spin? At least try and write a few thousand words and see what happened?

~

Whether or not I initially intended Ralph Bryson to be such a vile character I've no idea. Honestly. And don't ask me to tell you what the trigger for him was or where the idea of him came from because I haven't a clue. Writing about someone in authority abusing that authority wasn't exactly original — is anything? — but once it had popped into my head I couldn't shift it. The first questions to be answered required identification of the person, their profession, and the nature of their transgression. I thought about a politician but that was hackneyed — and Jeffrey Archer had recently exhausted that subject anyway. Then I asked myself who were the people we trusted most? Who did we place in a position where they could do unspeakable damage to us if they chose?

A doctor. Ralph Bryson was going to be a doctor. Overlaying that with the idea of writing the narrative in a form of stream-of-consciousness fit so well it seemed like a masterstroke: it would be the perfect way to describe the nature of his temptation, his depravity — the logic of it, if you like. His logic. I could let people into his mind, lay bare his compulsions, his addictions. It would be stimulating to write — and difficult to read. In more than one sense. For a while I played around with what kind of doctor Bryson should be: a psychiatrist perhaps, messing with people's minds; or a physiotherapist, messing with their bodies. I wondered about a geriatric specialist, but the patients would be too weak to fight back; or a paediatrician — too risky. And in any case, the vast majority of us don't come across those kinds of specialists.

If he was a GP he could be all kinds of doctor, whatever I wanted him to be.

- And in the end?

- In the end what?

- You know: sex, abuse. The nature of it.

Bryson was twisted. He didn't have one 'specialism' — if I can call it that... I didn't want him to be a sex maniac, partly because doing so would have made both he and the book too narrow; and *I* didn't want to be labelled either.

- You liked sex, though. It was your own 'specialism'.

He needed to be a predator, someone who revelled in others' weaknesses. He was a bully. Oh, charming and erudite on the outside — someone you'd happily introduce to your grandmother — but on the inside, a monster. That's what I was interested in: how monsters behaved, what made them a monster in the first place, how they justified their actions to themselves. Don't forget, in Martha I'd had my own close encounter with a monster. And getting inside his head, telling it from his perspective, that unfiltered and twisted stream of consciousness view... Tantalising!

By the time I decided to sell the concept to Declan I was already about a third of the way through the first draft. He thought it risky, edgy (he liked edgy things remember!); he appreciated the different nature of it, both style and content. So he went into bat for me without having the whole thing, started selling the idea, teasing Macmillan with the prospect of them having something groundbreaking on their list. He knew the buttons to press; *you casually say 'Booker' and some people start drooling* he said.

So they drooled; I got a decent advance. About eighteen months later *A Spoonful of Sugar* hit the bookshops. And then I waited.

- For what?

- You know for what: feedback, reviews, sales.

- In what order?

- Finally, a decent question!

And to which I'm not sure I have the perfect answer. Circumstance — i.e. what happened next — came to suggest that reviews were the most important; uppermost, if you like. Sales tend to follow reviews — both good and bad — not the other way round.

~

there's something about Frances Williams that constantly annoys me a long thin streak of a woman without any meaningful contours and a face that could cut paper or her nose could at least her voice too come to think of it a rasping one that gives you the impression she knows more than you about every topic under the sun and that includes what's wrong with her it's as if she's doing me a favour by coming to the surgery and allowing me to examine her as if she's offering herself up as a lab rat or a test case but there's nothing special about Mrs Williams not in the medical sense yes she's a unique piece of work but not medically she's just getting older and suffering from all the attendant nonsense that goes along with that and I see dozens of people like her every week sometimes every day and most of them are pleasant enough grateful enough and I think I can say I actually want to help most of them though there are a few I'd like to help in a different way and perhaps I already have so maybe I'll prescribe something for Mrs Williams that will put her out of my misery and maybe I'll hint to Morgan down at the Co-op ask him if he ever has something special made from cheap plywood and in the shape of a cigar tube because that would probably serve the purpose don't you think especially as she's hardly a contender for any of my more tender treatments and on that basis something to the point something conclusive would seem to be the only medication to prescribe and if there's still a Mr Williams then I'd be doing him a favour so maybe I should consider him too though I find it hard to believe that anyone could have the constitution to outlive her if they were in close-proximity for a number of years and so considering the wider picture makes me regret that I didn't recognise the invasiveness of her sooner and act sooner because I might have been able to save a life her husband's daily existence which is what I'm here for after all

~

If I was being modest or self-effacing I'd say the reviews were 'balanced'. But really they were almost universally good. People were taken aback by the shift in style, the dark nature of the material, its themes.

- 'Almost universally good'?

Russell Craig was 'old school'. No. Let's face it, Craig was just old. Nearly seventy when the book came out. He'd retired so many times people had lost count! Still punched out the odd review, maybe one a month, and was venerated in some circles. Craig's taste appealed to a certain 'Surrey demographic'.

Almost at the opposite end of the social spectrum, Morgan Harris was about ten years younger; a working class boy from the North East 'made good'. He leant on his accent and background to differentiate himself from the other hacks; he had a couple of monthly columns in papers and magazines that mattered; liked to pride himself on being able to give 'the layman's view' — which was all bollocks really. He was only interested in what made money and kept his name in the literary frame. Rumour had it that he wanted to be a Booker judge but kept getting passed over because he wasn't clever enough.

- Bitchy!

- Not my rumour, Bro.

Anyway, they both hated my book: Craig because he thought it some kind of Joycean pastiche, a cheap and vulgar imitation; and Harris because it was — and I quote — "inaccessible to the working man". Most good books aren't accessible to the average working man, don't you think?

I mean, come on.

Instantly, they had me thinking of Horberry. How could I not? But it was a parallel which held no water. That was then and this was now — and 'now' was significant. *A Spoonful of Sugar* was 'the second novel', the one to prove I was no one-hit-wonder. If it got panned, faced a groundswell of opinion against it, then there might not be the chance for a third. In that sense, Craig and Harris's negative views were an existential threat. But I believed in the book — and in the talent I'd demonstrated to have written the damn thing in the first place.

So, I had a choice: I could stay quiet or I could fight them. When Declan warned me that a few people were starting to listen to Craig and Harris, what choice did I have?

I want to call them out I remember saying to Declan. He was sceptical. *Why go looking for trouble? Their noise will die down.* I told him it was about more than noise: they were bullies hiding behind the shields of their publications; bullies who never took responsibility for their words. They'd got away with it for years. It was important someone made a stand. Exactly the thing I hadn't been able to do with Horberry.

- No such thing as bad publicity?

- Shut up.

Whether he could see my motivation wasn't really about bringing them to justice I don't know. Self-preservation can take many forms — including attack being the best form of defence and all that.

We kicked around how we might be able to engineer an encounter and what form such an encounter might take. Duncan was all in favour of something low-key and low-risk, where we'd do minimal damage to ourselves if it all went pear-shaped. Protection of a different kind. But he could see I was coming at it from the opposite perspective; if we won, the damage would be all on their side. *Let's make some noise of our own* I suggested.

I'd already drafted the open letter I planned to send to both their rags. 'Incendiary' was how he described it. And it was. *You'll have painted them into a corner. They'll either have to recant or come out fighting.* I wanted to know which he thought most likely. *It depends what they believe they have to lose — and how likely they think they are to win. Make no mistake, if you send the letter then that's where we'll be: 'winners' and 'losers' territory.* Which is exactly where I wanted to be. I wanted them rattled, to know they were going to be in a scrap. And I wanted to win. Declan thought Craig was likely to agree to cross swords simply because he was old enough not to be risking anything material — and because he thought he was bullet-proof. Declan was less certain of Harris. *But if Craig says 'yes' then he'll drag Harris along with him. Strength in numbers; typical bully-boy tactics.*

So we sent the letter. And not only to their publications but also a slightly modified version to a couple of other magazines. I didn't want Craig and Harris to be able to duck the challenge. In effect it was an invitation to a duel; turning it down would be nothing other than an act of cowardice.

Things moved with surprising swiftness. We heard back from Harris's paper first, then from Craig himself. He claimed to be "incensed" by the accusations in my letter: of course he knew what he was talking about; of course he wasn't hamstrung by ancient thinking; and of course he could recognise good and inventive writing when he saw it — which mine wasn't. Soon after, Declan was contacted by Jessica Goddard, host of a well-regarded late-night television show which survived on an eclectic mix of contemporary middle-class smut and highbrow art. *It's a blend that shouldn't work* he said, *but it does thanks to Jessica. And she's offered to referee your debate.*

She was an obvious choice. Craig was an old friend (rumour had it, an old flame) who appeared regularly on her show casting pearls before swine. With him wanting to have a public rant at *A Spoonful of Sugar*, she said I'd offered him the perfect opportunity. Then she assured Declan of her neutrality.

If I was nervous at any point, it was probably at the precise moment I knew the encounter was set. Being able to fix it to her show and give our coming together a date made all the difference. With the recording just a week away, it was a nervousness I couldn't afford to last too long.

Once it was all over Harris and Craig subsequently accused me of walking onto the set drunk.

- As if!

- As if what? As if you were there?

~

Everyone made too much of it — especially the way they linked Russell and I together as if we were some kind of double act: 'Craig and Harris'. But double acts tend to be comedians, don't they — Morecambe & Wise, Hinge & Bracket — or singing duos. But we couldn't sing and we weren't comedians — even if that's what Charles imagined we were.

But it wasn't being thought of in that way which bothered me; rather it was losing my individuality. And being 'the junior partner' implied (for some people, at any rate) that I was Russell's lackey. Which I most certainly wasn't; not before, during, or after.

Don't get me wrong, in a way I quite liked the old boy. He was something of a legend, of course. But there were people (and

I'm not saying I was one of them) who thought he was on his way out, had had his day. There was a new breed snapping at his heels — and soon enough snapping at my heels too!

I think from his perspective he saw me as riding shotgun for him, running interference, playing second fiddle, offering moral support. He'd made it clear from the beginning that the interview on Jessica's show was his gig; he was the star attraction. Which was funny because it was soon evident that Charles thought he was the star!

And what did I think?

Well, I didn't take it as seriously as the other two, that's for sure — even if Charles turned up half-pissed. It was deadly serious for Russell, which was one of the reasons he got so riled; Charles taking the opposite stance and giving the impression the whole thing was just a bit of fluff was the other — even if that was just the drink talking. Russell was clearly wrong; his 'fucker' comment demonstrated just how badly he'd misjudged the situation and, I suppose, his adversary…

And Charles? I never really had anything against the guy. He clearly had some talent — well, he's proven as much, hasn't he? — but back then? He was either going to make it or he would end up as cannon fodder. Thanks to being so pissed off by Charles calling him out, Russell had mistakenly prejudged the outcome. Me? I just went along for the ride.

~

They're calling it an honourable draw Declan said a few days later; *I've had a letter suggesting a truce.* I laughed. *They're running scared. They're trying to save face — but they don't matter anyway.* The way he looked at me over the top of his pint, I knew he was just playing the game. *Oh? Why not?* I took a theatrical pause. *Because they lost — and because what the numbers say is the most important thing.*

The whole enterprise hadn't been about sales of course, but something more important. Yet where else could one look for evidence, for vindication? Jessica's show was hardly a mega draw — a few hundred thousand viewers perhaps — but there were snippets subsequently shown elsewhere. *They ran a clip on 'This Morning',* Declan offered suddenly. *Really?* I couldn't conceal my delight. *Which bit?* His smile told me before his words did: *Where you enraged Craig so much — the repetition of 'fossil' — that he swore. They bleeped out 'you upstart fucker' of course.* I was reminded of 'upstart crow'.

- That was funny; I'll give you that.

- Thanks.

So perhaps he's now a little less of a national treasure. We'd both laughed. *And the numbers?* The way Declan was stringing me along told me the news was good. *A significant up-tick: a little the day after the show, and then again once 'This Morning' had run the clip.* I'd smiled. *So we're vindicated? The existential crisis is over?* Declan finished his beer. *There was a little noise about your referencing Joyce — some people thought that pretentious — but I think you're in the clear. Onwards and upwards!*

~

I can't deny that for a short while I revelled in my victory. There was something gladiatorial about it. In a way, it was almost primitive. I knew Declan would be working in the background to smooth things over — the evidence of him having done so coming a few years later when Harris wrote some nice things about my work, including *A Spoonful of Sugar.* Maybe he felt able to do so because Craig was dead by then — though to be frank I don't think I was aware of that, and I certainly didn't care. About either of them.

One of the interesting aspects of the whole episode — especially the way the three of us bandied words around before, during, and after our skirmish — was how flexible our weapons could be. The same word — like 'inventive' or 'modern', 'fresh' or 'Joycean' — suggested something subtly different depending on who uttered it, the context in which it appeared, and how it was said. Not that this was news to me — after all, I'd been on the receiving end of multiple declarations of 'love' over the previous decade. Surely there's no more interpreted — and *mis*interpreted — word than *that* in the history of language! But our brief encounter was akin to a refresher course in intent and translation, a reminder that 'meaning' was compound and complex. It was almost as if a word on its own was vaguely worthless; as if all its power came from whether it was spoken softly or loudly, aggressively or passively; whether someone said something with their arms crossed or not, or whether they were standing or sitting. And it was influenced by the web of words around it too; what came immediately before and after.

Years before, when I'd first started out, maybe I used to think that words were somehow sacrosanct, rigorously defined; that when you wrote 'harsh' it could only mean one thing, be open to a single interpretation. Maybe that's how we start to learn language; how we *have* to learn language. Naïve, when you think about it. Maybe such a rudimentary belief made much of my early work — my attempts before *Tainted Harvest* (or even including *Harvest*, who knows?) — nothing more than one-dimensional. For a reader, something lacking depth may mean they always know what is going on or what is intended. More 'tell' than 'show'. Hardly challenging. But *A Spoonful of Sugar* — both the book and the subsequent public spat — was the true beginning of me going beyond the veneer of words.

- Or at least that's what you say now.

- It's what I thought then.

- Really? But you didn't tell Declan that.

- Why should I? This was about craft, my relationship with my tools; it had nothing to do with him.

- Interesting angle.

- Why so?

- Because of what came next.

'Sparse', 'lean', 'taut'; those were the things Declan liked about my work, and in saying as much he was pairing those labels with his own definitions for them. If my understanding was different (and perhaps it was) that didn't stop him — stop *us* — from behaving as if we were communicating under the auspices of a common language. He'd say 'taut' and I'd nod knowingly; a favour he returned if I said 'sparse'.

Of course, on one level we weren't sharing the same language at all.

And that was suddenly interesting to me: the discord in words people use, irrespective of the flaws in a supposedly common understanding. That joke about the British and the Americans being divided by a common language isn't really a joke. I was determined to learn from my Craig/Harris encounter, and if a renewed appreciation of the deceptive nature of words was the one thing I took from it then so be it. That and an increased confidence that I was now able to weave them together better than ever before.

- Or lie more convincingly.

- You would see it that way. How could you not?

I suppose I'd always assumed that lying meant telling a story which wasn't true. A false narrative. I could tell you that I once had tea at Buckingham Palace, but that would be a lie; it never happened, even though I had presented it as fact. Common or garden lying I suppose. It's what everyone does, isn't it?

Yet now I had come to see that words themselves told lies too. Use the same word in two similar narratives — but subtly change the context in one — and you can easily move from truth to lie. Irony. Sarcasm. Say one thing and mean another — and all the while remaining ostensibly true to the words themselves. It was a delicious kind of overlay. Craig, Harris and I had been jousting in that way throughout our encounter. Nothing so bland or obvious as uttering "with all due respect" when there is a total *absence* of respect, but adopting more subtle nuances in how we layered on the words.

Come to think of it, Craig may have said *with all due respect* at one point — perhaps that had been the beginning of his descent to *you upstart fucker*.

If you think about Craig's journey that evening from untouchable national treasure towards foul-mouthed bully-boy, there was a further and entirely related lesson to be harvested. He had been steered that way — if not forced, come to think of it — by the power of words. No blows had been struck, nor had there been any lies told (which is interesting in the overall context of the event, isn't it?); we had simply exchanged contrary viewpoints. Robustly, of course, and not without heat. But the damage? The blows were delivered by using words like 'fossil' — and damage proven when he said 'fucker'.

Luckily I was on the right side of the argument.

- You mean simply because you won?

- What are you trying to say?

- Only that you could have been wrong, and Craig right.

And being on the right side meant I had the power with me. The power of the language.

I realised — either then or soon after (and that's before Matty chimes in again) — the weapons words could be, especially if you could fashion them appropriately. Words spoken as well as written. For the first time I think I understood that they were not simply vehicles for stories, for truths or lies, but that they could be wielded to reach further, and do so much more. Profess 'love' and you might be being genuine or telling a lie, or — depending on how you did so, how the word was delivered, the context in which it made its debut — something far more sinister.

Bryson was sinister, and not just because of what he did. He told truths to his patients, and to some of them he told lies; but each and every time he was manipulating them, giving out coded messages, weakening the people he wanted to weaken, and — whether being honest or not — finding ways to abuse the ones he wanted to abuse. And always words came first. *I'm afraid I've some bad news...* Truth or lie? Did he have any news at all, and if so, was it 'bad'? And was he ever 'afraid'? How were you supposed to know about any of it?

Well, you were supposed to know not only because you trusted a man in his position, but because you put your faith in the words he spoke. And from my perspective as a purveyor of narrative, even more powerful was that you trusted the man who'd written those words in the first place...

At some point I think I felt as if *I* was Bryson, in his shoes, his position of power. I had a weapon I could wield — no, *was* wielding — and if people made the decision to read what I had written, well, they were making themselves vulnerable. Entirely.

- What are you saying? That you were superior, in control?

- ...

- Or that you're Bryson — or God?

- 'God-like' perhaps. But powerful, certainly. And in many ways in control over what a reader might think or feel.

- Or believe.

I was beginning to have an idea of what I might be able to do.

I think Joyce understood all aspects of that power. Stephen was searching for it, and Bloom was confused by it. But Molly? Molly had found it, knew how to wield it. Joyce gave her the power of a new language, a mythology in which truth and lies were all mixed together, where words became unreliable handmaidens — at least as far as the reader was concerned. And maybe as far as Bloom was concerned too. But Molly…

Being able to tame words, to rip them from any conventional notion of truth, to have them serve multiple masters at the same time — truth and lie, writer and reader — isn't that what mythology and fable are all about?

Okay maybe the penny didn't drop immediately after my Craig and Harris encounter, but soon enough things began to slot into place. I'd debunked one myth — that Craig was the 'national treasure' he saw himself as being — and had begun to solidify another: my own. Not as a kind of 'Jack the Giant-slayer', but as someone who had something to offer; someone who needed to be taken seriously. The notion I had in mind — embryonic back in 1989, I'll admit — was that I could be a creator of myths and not merely characters like Bryson. The fictional 'me' I was becoming attached to — or detached from — and who I was keen to cultivate, could become myth too; there was a convolution of truth and lie to be ravelled (rather than unravelled).

- You wanted to become like Bryson.

- How so?

- To manipulate people.

- Benevolently of course, through what I wrote.

- Is that all?

- What do you mean?

- Manipulation solely through your writing, that's what I'm asking. Had you any concept of a line not to be crossed? Or didn't you think you needed one, some separation — especially when you consider what came later.

Bull

1991 - 1993

It was time to take my new-found understanding for a spin. 1991 and all was well with the world. If you think about it, I'd come a long way in a relatively short period of time; or that's how it seemed. There was nothing specific I was working towards, no pre-planned stopping points on my journey, no itinerary of things to see or do. I had no 'bucket list' — but I suppose a list of sorts was building.

- Of which this endeavour may be the last entry.

- But only if you see a list as a finite selection of items to be 'crossed off'; things you know you want to do, so you slavishly work through them.

And if I'd kept a list (of experiences I'd both had *and* wanted to have mind you, including things to write) then I would have been *adding* to it constantly, not only the wishes, but the things achieved: finding things out, like the ability of words to lie; the Craig and Harris episode; or my life with Hazel. Maybe there was an inevitable bleeding between the two, past and future: finding something out, then wanting to put that new knowledge to good use. A virtuous spiral. That's how it felt at the beginning of another decade.

Declan was already asking his favourite question — "what next?" — *because*, he said, *we need to strike while the iron's hot.* I knew what he meant, but I had nothing specific in mind.

Or rather I did, but I was keeping it under wraps for a while.

So I suggested a collection of stories, partly to feed the machine, and partly to keep the wolf from the door. I had some post-*Avalanche* material — including *Dark Corner* — and I was bullish enough to commit to being able to churn out the requisite new stories to make a reasonably-sized volume.

- Which was cocky of you.

- I was feeling confident. And why shouldn't I have been?

And I felt it right that *Dark Corner* should now be published; I felt I could take the emotional 'hit'. I even suggested creating prose versions of *Harvest* and *Sunbathing*, the bulk of the work having already been done. Declan quite liked the ensemble idea; suggested it might create a 'self-perpetuating circle of publicity'. In some respects he was like a faithful terrier: throw him a stick and he'd chase after it, then bring it back.

- Hardly complimentary.

- He wouldn't mind me saying so.

- Well, he's hardly in a position to complain.

- That's correct, of course — though remember, I only let you in under sufferance.

- This isn't sufferance, it's guilt.

So the short story collection became my background project for the year. I sent Declan the first draft just before Christmas. We faffed with it a bit after that, but there wasn't too much to be done: when stories are shorter there are fewer loose ends to worry about, fewer characters to refine; the checks and balances are different.

And oddly, that lack of faffing was similar for my 'big' project too, the one I revealed to Declan in the Autumn — and only then because I had enough to show him. And too much to turn my back on.

In deciding to 'reshape' Shakespeare I hadn't needed to worry about plot or characters. You know who's who in *King Lear*; you know what happens in *Hamlet*. That wasn't the point. The challenge I set myself (maybe not too dissimilar to the prose version of *Tainted Harvest*) was to take something created in one form then translate or transpose it into another. *Ode on a Grecian Urn* and all that. They call it 'ekphrastic' these days. It's trendy.

It might have been a bridge too far, of course; that was the risk. Declan's initial reaction was *Are you Crazy?* — which I plainly wasn't. But I had this urge to test myself, my craft, the tricks I'd learned. And I wanted to weave all my new knowledge about words and truth and lies into something already existing — already written even! — to see how far I could push things, to see what I could get away with. These weren't going to be like-for-like translations. Far from it. People would go into the stories with their minds already made up because they knew the original. Foreknowledge would give them expectations as to what the characters would say and do — but I wanted to unsettle all that. Keep reasonably close to the bones of the narratives, yes, but then add in a little twist here and there to unsettle the reader, to force them to answer questions they hadn't been expecting to be posed. And maybe ask questions of themselves too.

- But to rewrite Shakespeare?

- I know! Wild idea, wasn't it?

Though I'd argue that it wasn't a rewrite, not in the literal sense (and already that may be a lie!) but rather an attempt to demystify, reshape, tame, reimagine.

- But, again, why?

That was Declan's second question. Or one of them. I told him I was partly paying homage — and partly settling a debt. And that remembering how badly Shakespeare had been taught at school, it was also an attempt to offer a degree of inspiration usually denied kids just at the very point when they need to learn the kinds of lessons Shakespeare put front-and-centre.

That was the moral view if you like.

- Or the pompous one.

But I was also doing it *because* it was Shakespeare — and because I felt compelled to test myself, to see if I could pull off the magic trick. I'd already taken a run at Joyce remember... And I didn't want to be known for *Dominance, Spoonful,* and a few short stories; nor to be seen as some minor celebrity thanks to a clash on a late-night tv show where some old guy said 'fucker' and got bleeped out. It was partly because of that incident I feared *Spoonful* — the book itself — might end up being overlooked, overwhelmed by lazy categorisation. Don't forget, I was in my early forties now. I already had a sense the clock was ticking. Or the window was closing. You know. There would come a point where people would cease to be interested in me because I was getting old. I'd got my foot in the door and, by God, I was determined to keep it there.

At least that.

~

On one level Charles was not an easy client. Oh, he had lots going for him, of course: drive, an insatiable appetite to try things out, bravery — but bravery to the point of recklessness sometimes. That episode with Craig and Harris for example. After, he was never going to stand still or rest on his laurels — which was great from my perspective because I knew there would always be something fresh coming down the pipe. Kept me on my toes too.

But all of that — drive, appetite and bravery — meant risk was never that far away, and the Shakespeare idea seemed off the scale. If it went wrong then he could become a laughing stock; that was the risk. I tried to persuade him against it, but he was set; so the collection of short stories (which, if I'm honest, I also didn't really want to do) was a kind of insurance policy. We needed to demonstrate he was a serious writer just in case the Bard adaptations blew up in his face.

He got away with it in the end. Or rather, we did. The books didn't fall on their arse; they opened up his work to a new tranche of readers; they made him more interesting, I suppose. Think about it; in relatively short order, **Spoonful,** *a collection of shorts (including* **Dark Corner***), and the Shakespeare re-tellings. Who else would have attempted something like that? No-one I knew. And like I say, he got away with it.*

I managed to get someone to give me a second opinion before we finalised the Shakespeare project; I wanted verification. There was no point going to a scholar — they'd laugh it out of court — so I picked someone you might describe as 'a man of letters': proven, respected etcetera. He thought the work interesting, but marginal; he could see merit in the writing, but thought the book frivolous. He didn't really understand why Charles was so set on doing it. I asked him flat out, "if <u>you</u> had to choose between publishing and not, what would you do?" His response was unequivocal: "I'd publish — but only because I thought **Spoonful** *was really good."*

Was that faint praise? Damning or otherwise, I didn't know — but it was enough for me.

Charles discovered I'd sought a second opinion (I can't remember whether I'd volunteered it or not) but I never let him know who my reader was. That might have involved opening a whole new can of worms, and I had no desire to make things more complicated. Although he was unhappy, I refused to divulge the reader's identity. Charles actually met him much later and they got on famously — perhaps because he failed to make the connection. Maybe I'd worried about nothing, but when you're mitigating risk...

~

As far as process was concerned the writing was relatively straightforward. I would read a play a few times; if someone had made a film of it or there was a recording of an RSC performance, I'd try and hunt those out. Then I'd decide on the angle I was going to take, the twist I would apply — the 'slant' view — and then go from there.

I wanted the stories to be ten to fifteen thousand words long, partly because that was long enough, and partly because an intelligent reader would have sufficient advanced knowledge to render lots of scene-setting unnecessary. For putting a book together I figured six plays would do the trick, but I worked on seven just in case: *Lear, Hamlet, Macbeth, Julius Caesar, Henry V, The Merchant*, and *The Shrew*. Perhaps mine was akin to a theatre director's experience; choosing the context for my versions was a great challenge — and in a good way. *Henry* against the backdrop of twentieth century party politics was fun (in the previous couple of years Thatcher had lost the plot, there were protests against the Poll Tax), and *Hamlet* set in the cut-throat world of a firm of ex-Yuppie management consultants seemed like a good idea.

I'll admit some of my choices were more successful than others — and more than once Declan warned me not to get too close to Brecht and *Arturo Ui*. Eventually he'd been persuaded as to the project, but didn't want me to deliver pastiche.

So I drafted, he read and gave feedback; I redrafted, and then Declan had someone else (he never told me who) provide independent feedback. Then came a final version.

- So it was a year of stories.

- '91? And much of '92 as well. Yet following on from the grind of *Spoonful* (because that had been intense!) it was almost relaxing.

- You were upset though.

- Upset? Why?

- Because Declan never told you who that second reader was.

- Okay, maybe I was a bit pissed off at the time.

- Was that the beginning of the end? Like Thatcher?

- With Declan? I don't think so. Maybe. Who knows?

He was more disappointed with the outcome of my big project than I was, certainly in terms of reviews. Oddly enough, sales were pretty good, aided by the PR of a few high profile independent schools taking the collection as an adjunct to their Shakespeare curriculum. A few people seemed intrigued to find out how I'd answered the 'what next?' question, to see if what came after *Spoonful* was going to be as divisive. In some senses it was of course. The new stories were perfectly palatable. 'Bite-sized'. Which seemed to make them popular. And a number of people commented on how well-written they were; 'coherent' was a term often used, presumably reflecting on my handling of the source material.

But there were naysayers. There were always going to be; the purist brigade who regarded any tampering with The Bard as sacrilegious. They thought I'd gone too far, was taking the piss. For a small minority — a very small minority (who'd probably hated *Spoonful* too) — it was further demonstration that I had no talent of my own and was simply pinching from the greats. 'On the shoulders of giants', remember? But luckily these were in the minority. At the other extreme, some people wondered whether it ought to be nominated for the Costa or something. MacMillan weren't keen.

Overall I think what shone through was the fact that people applauded the endeavour. There was a degree of kudos to be harvested from simply 'having a go'. They admired my balls. No-one else had attempted what I had — at least not publicly and to such an extent. Oh, they'd played with settings in the theatre, but they'd left the words alone. And now I'd come along and pretty much ditched most of the words and just kept the scaffolding, wrapped a new skin around that. *Henry* and *Hamlet* garnered most praise; I think that was because they were contemporary, edgy. There was a growing penchant for the political in the arts — and a backlash against the City-centric Tory 'me first' mentality. People had become only too willing to wade-in and diss Thatcher's legacy. One or two prominent Labour MPs offered soundbites for the cover of the second edition. Declan had the wisdom to politely turn them down.

- And Craig and Harris?

- What did they say, you mean? Almost nothing.

Craig made passing reference to the book by trumpeting the fact that "Shakespeare lives on!", suggesting my motivation had been — as with Joyce — to 'undo' great literature, and that I'd failed. I guess in his eyes I'd doubled-down on *Spoonful*.

But that wasn't the game at all. Anyone who thought I'd been on the attack was missing the point entirely. My work may not have been a kowtowing tribute or a fawning over the original, but in a way it was paying its own kind of homage. And I was trying to open doors and not close them; the doors in readers' minds — even if "read this and then go read the original and see how great it is" wasn't a claim many people swallowed. But I'd like to think that wasn't so far from the source of my motivation.

~

"Why did he resign?"

"He didn't resign." He watched his words land, saw realisation dawning on Horatio.

"So he sacked him?" The only other option.

The smile was only partly playful. "He didn't sack him; he 'let him go'."

"Fuck it, that's just semantics!"

"Maybe — but you know how important appearance is to Claude. Semantics is one of his favourite weapons. That's why he's so good at wooing customers, lying to them."

"And stabbing colleagues in the back."

It was a statement which proved Hamlet's insinuation had hit the mark. Knowing Horatio was firmly on his side, he could afford to let the assertion go unacknowledged. "It's a skill that's enabled him to get where he is."

"The top of the tree?"

"If you want to see it that way…" He paused, walked to the window, stared down across London Bridge station and into the city. On the pavements below, figures went about their business almost as ghosts might; in cars, drivers wrestled with the afternoon traffic striving not to miss appointments — or rushing to escape them and head home. At the foot of their building he could make out two men walking toward the entrance, a tell-tale light brown suit clearly visible even from nineteen floors up. Rose and Stern, presumably on their way to meet with Claude; they were his favourite 'fixers'.

"How else?" Horatio checked his watch.

Seeing the time-check, he let the question go. "Need to be somewhere?"

"Project meeting in five."

"And after?"

"Nothing I can't shift."

"Here just after six? I'll let you have my theory — and then I'll buy you a drink."

~

But look, I'm not stupid. What I did probably made no significant difference. In the end, I mean. Thirty years on and Shakespeare is still causing terror in schools. And people still can't wrap their heads around Joyce.

- So it was a failure.

- A failure?

- The whole escapade. Did you achieve what you set out to?

- I think so.

- Elaborate.

- Must I?

- This is your gig, remember.

- The book sold; I made money. Let's start right there. If you're desperate for me to tick things off…

- What I want doesn't come into it.

- Right. Think about what happened even before then… Look, I had an idea and was able to see it through.

- Another tick.

- Of course. But a bigger one than the money. The most important one.

- A little self-indulgent, perhaps?

That's what a few people said. Mainly those who thought I was on some kind of ego trip, or trying to destroy the classics. Neither of which was true. Obviously.

It was the task, the craft. Taking learned lessons, remember, then weaving them into something else; using words to twist the original characters around a little. Blurring truth and lies. I still wish I'd tackled *Romeo and Juliet*. I can imagine a version where Romeo's not as principled, where Juliet's a bit of a tart, and the Friar is most definitely *not* on their side. *That* would have been fun to write!

- You still could.

- Ha! That's a bit like suggesting Jessie Owens could still win an Olympic 100m — and he's been dead over forty years.

- Didn't they ask you to produce a second volume?

- We talked about it. They'd made enough dosh out of the first for it to be viable. And oddly Declan was keen. Maybe he thought it would be easy money.

- Another misjudgement.

If there's one common thread to my work it's that I don't repeat — and I don't count rewrites of *Harvest* or *Sunbathing* as repeats by the way. Try something, prove you can do it, move on to the next thing, the next idea, the next style.

Recently someone said I was like a literary shark: I had to keep moving forward in order to stay alive. I quite liked that; thought it was perceptive.

- And flattering.

- Shut up. Surely my track record demonstrates as much.... Do something fresh, learn from it, move on.

- Could almost be a philosophy for life.

- And if it was, it wouldn't be a bad one.

- I said life, not work.

- I heard you.

Most people seemed to miss that on one level what I'd done had been nothing more than simply continue a tradition. Writers have been at it for years: taking the old then reshaping and reimagining it. Where's the difference with what Joyce did with the story of the Trojan hero and what I did with my slant on *Hamlet* or *Lear*? Or what Shakespeare himself did to old stories once he'd got his hands on them? What was Joyce doing with *Ulysses* if not holding up a mirror to mythology and 'great literature'? And a distorting mirror at that. He took something, examined it, twisted it, made it into something else. Even the words themselves.

People miss the irony there too. Joyce's sideswipe at how things were (or used to be) eventually morphed into great literature in its own right. His work joined the pantheon, became normalised, lauded. I wonder what he'd make of that now. It's either mind-boggling or ridiculously ironic. Of course that wasn't my intention, to create 'great literature'. I don't think you can set out to do that because, let's face it, it's a gift entirely out of your control. It's bestowed on you by readers. Or that's what we're led to believe, that they're the king-makers in all this: readers, academics, reviewers. Oh, you can hone your talent, try to influence (though that's not the explicit job of the writer, mind) but you can't cajole or buy their endorsement.

I'm kidding. That's not entirely true.

There are those on the periphery who, for a few Euros, will put their name to some snappy soundbite just to get it on a cover — especially if they think the book is going to sell well. It's dishonest activity which, in a way, has absolutely nothing to do with the book itself.

- Have you ever done that?

- I don't think I've ever endorsed anything.

- What about Declan?

- He knew a few 'names' whose palms were open to greasing.

- And did he? Did you benefit from his 'lubrication'?

- You'd have to ask him.

- You know I can't. And on at least two levels.

- The third being?

- That you wouldn't let me.

The facts of the matter were plain enough. Maybe that's where the focus should be: my books sold well; on balance, the reviews were positive; by and large the stories did what I set out for them to do. And they didn't become — nor were they intended to become — 'great literature'. Not to my mind, anyway.

~

Success? Having been to the well once — and given there was so much more that could be harvested — a second set of 're-interpretations' seemed like a good idea. Yes, I'd changed my tune, I acknowledge that; but we'd got away with it, and I found myself wondering what else Charles might be able to do with more of the Bard's canon.

And the publishers were keen. They'd already begun to map-out how they'd market volume number two; they could see a way forward based on a slightly different marketing tack, a new form factor for the books. Give them a second volume and they'd reissue the first in a new edition — that's what they promised me. And maybe even a third. Or fourth. It was the kind of carrot that doesn't get dangled very often.

I'll be honest, the proposal sounded great to me — from my perspective, I mean. All I'd have to do was to be the link-man between them and Charles — and I was convinced he could run off a volume a year for the next two or three years without any trouble. Easy money for everyone. There were writers who'd simply jump at such a chance. You can think of a few who've none nothing but churn out the same old rubbish for twenty or thirty years and ended up making a good living from doing so, thank you very much…

But not Charles. His demons were his drive and appetite, that need to do something fresh, take risks. I didn't expect his reaction to the proposal to 'go again' to be so radical, negative;

he was vehemently opposed. The more I pushed, the more he resisted.

I probably pushed too hard. Or maybe the damage had already been done by then, even if I couldn't see how or when the fracture had occurred. The second reader for Spoonful maybe. Not that I saw the chasm opening up, not straight away. But soon enough. And with Charles there was no going back. He had this thing about 'moving forwards'; once he'd made his mind up about something there was no back-tracking. Error or failure, challenge or opportunity; these were often met with confrontation. Don't forget Craig and Harris. I didn't want to end up blackballed like them. So later, when it came to putting up a fight, I didn't bother.

And after?

I've painted a picture. You can apply the bones of it to all that followed if you want to; I'm not going to mark your card.

~

- And lessons?

- What do you mean, 'and lessons'?

- What did you learn? You're always so boastful about what you've learned, how an experience allows you to 'grow'.

- Am I? … Well if I am that's simply because it's true. You could call it 'the Shark Philosophy': keep moving forward.

- Sharks eat people too you know.

- Not as many as you'd think.

- Did you eat people along the way, brother mine? In addition to me that is.

- I would like to debate that one.

- What about Declan? Or Hazel? Or even Craig?

Writers are essentially consumers. Not in the sense that we buy things in order to eat or use them, not in the physical sense anyway. Or maybe we're more 'absorbers' than 'consumers'. We take our experiences — or others' experiences — and transform them into something else: a panoply of written words. And it's that filtered, enhanced, disguised, reshaped product we offer up for others to consume.

Surely I've proven that much: Valerie's rape; the evil Bryson; the learnings from my clash with Craig and Harris.

- And me?

We scavenge. We can't help ourselves. It's wonderfully compulsive; it goes with the territory, is part of the job description… If we didn't do that then what the hell would we have to write about? I scavenged Shakespeare; so what? I've done far worse that that. Or perhaps I should say I've been far more inventive, original, and — before you say anything — 'personal'. Like Bryson. But my Bard stories were impersonal. They were all about craft and proving a theory: that I could do something fresh; that I could handle slippery words in a different way.

Maybe it was just a magic trick. Maybe it's all just a magic trick. But yes, there were learnings too. Mainly in the request for a repeat. Volume Two. It was a clamour that grew more insistent until I put a stop to it. That told me a lot — mainly about the business. Or entirely about the business and those in it.

If I'd ever felt like some kind of hero in defeating Craig and Harris — and if in writing the short stories (both books, I suppose) I had a sense of being in control — then soon enough I realised I wasn't. Others were the king-makers. Up to that point I'd assumed the gift of coronation resided solely with my readers, starting with those who years before had sat through *Harvest* and clapped at the end — and certainly not with people like Horberry, Craig and Harris. But readers *don't* have the power. They have no more power than I have control. They're told what to read, steered in a direction — in the same way as 'the machine' tried to tell me what to write.

This new lesson — another twist or an ending-beginning on the journey — wasn't about the craft but about the machine. And about those who were pulling the strings. On reflection, I recognised I'd already had a glimpse of that with Craig and Harris; but when pressure was applied for me to pull a second rabbit from the Shakespearean story-hat… Maybe the penny dropped then.

On one level that was shocking. It was like playing chess thinking you were the queen or some other powerful piece only to discover you were a mere pawn. Not only that, the board wasn't uniform and the rules of the game were fluid and could change on you just like that: "I didn't know a knight could make that move!"

You go into the process, the industry, in good faith, thinking you know how it all works, believing what you're told, that there's a set of rules to which everyone adheres. And then, wham! If I have to give Craig credit for anything then it was knowing how to play the game — especially understanding when and how the rules changed. He'd bend with them; he'd deliver what was requested in the way it was requested, the manner of it. That was the secret of his longevity; or at least part of it.

Write another volume, Declan said. *It's easy money. Think about what you could do with 'Romeo' or 'Coriolanus' or 'The Tempest'. It would cement your reputation.*

I wondered what sort of reputation he had in mind. And that maybe he couldn't see I believed I already had one.

Horses

1994 - 1995

Writing is a carnivorous process. Did I say that already? Although writers are carnivores in their own way — that notion of consumption or absorption of people and stories, myths and legend — we are also consumed ourselves. I'm reminded of that scene in *King Kong* when the tribal villagers offer Ann Darrow up to the big ape. It's a bit fanciful I know, but being a writer can leave you feeling a little as Ann must have felt — especially if you look at the industry through a commercial lens.

Declan's *Write another volume* was akin to he and the publishers wanting to string me up and make me a human sacrifice. Or at least that was how I saw it.

Of course we're partial to the odd sacrifice. We indulge all the time; it makes us feel virtuous, special. We commit ourselves to a project, an idea, a deadline, and we become absorbed by it; everything else becomes secondary, subservient.

- Hazel saw that. She told you.

- But maybe I didn't hear her or couldn't see it at the time. And even if I had, would anything have changed?

- Has it changed now?

But it's more than self-sacrifice, this process of creation: it's about 'becoming' too. The new version of myself I was creating — that fictional 'me' — was a by-product of the process. Or of *my* process and all my projects.

No. More than that, it was a *necessary* part. If you are going to be forced into giving yourself up for the consumption of others, then you can't afford to give them all of you, your essence, otherwise what would be left? Especially if you failed — or if Kong chewed you up and then spat you out.

I think that's what Craig and Harris were trying to do. Or that was their raison d'être. They saw themselves as 'the beasts' who held the power over life and death via their columns — and they'd assumed I would simply succumb. Another victim, chosen on a whim perhaps.

I've seen people who have suffered in such a way: mainly one-hit-wonders who've fallen by the wayside, unable to follow-on from an initial success; or those who have tried to repeat a trick only for the public — or the business — to see through them. Husks; writers become has-beens, unable to take the next step. Dead in the water. Which I swore would never be me. Maybe that's why I always needed to try new things, not to repeat. Shark, remember.

It might have been as much about staying one step ahead as anything else. And trying to retain control. Maybe I thought that the only person who could make me a king was me, my fictitious 'me'.

- And which are you now?

- Isn't it obvious?

- I'm sure there's some clever and witty comment waiting in the wings, something about getting the monkey off your back.

- You're probably right — but being right is hardly your forte.

As soon as people in the business start to talk about symbiosis you know you're in trouble; publishers and Agents dangle the carrot about being aligned, wanting the same thing. In the beginning your Agent is batting for you because it's in their interest to do so; but once you've a foot in the door, as soon as you're published and successful, then you become someone else's property. At that point their allegiance shifts because the power shifts. What once belonged to the Agent evaporates, is transferred to the publisher, and in order to remain in the game, to stay 'relevant', the Agent switches sides. They have to.

- And that's based on?

- Declan, and his *Write another volume.*

- That's a pretty small sample size, if I may be so bold.

- Oh, don't you worry. I've seen it often enough to regard it as a truth, all those writing knights who might well have survived had their squires not swapped sides at the first commercial opportunity.

And I could name names too, but what's the point? Most were of my generation — and most long since dead. And for those that aren't? Too late to stir things up now. They've all gone on to do other things, follow other professions, bemoan what might have been. Those who still scribble do so — I don't know — out of a sense of duty or habit, happy enough to cling to the dying embers of that first book and the promise it once represented.

None of that was me — not in the sense of having only one book, nor in the sense of such a fate being something for which I'd settle.

Mind you, I didn't know what I'd write next, only what I wouldn't. Declan pestered; I told him not to worry, to take a break. And all the while I was beginning to tout myself directly to other publishers. Quietly mind. My fictional self took on the mantle of 'wide boy', a salesman; I wanted to see if I had accumulated enough brownie points, established sufficient cachet and knowledge of how things worked, for me to be my own agent and 'cut out the middle-man'.

It was also a test of course, mainly of my standing in the industry. It had nothing to do with ability — anyone's — and everything to do with control. For a while I even toyed with the idea of setting up a little publishing business myself, or establishing a relationship a bit like that Eliot fostered with Faber; but that felt a step too far. At least at that point in time.

- Steady on.

- What do you mean?

- Ideas above your station, bro.

- Fuck off.

People were interested, though there were subtle variations in how they viewed the prospect. Commonality was clear though: they all wanted to know "what next?" so they could decide whether they'd make any money or not. And they were also interested in *how* I proposed to make any arrangement work. Well that proved to be something of a minefield! Inevitably the exploratory discussions revolved around numbers: percentages, print runs, distribution, marketing and the like. Those were concrete things and could largely be derived from historical evidence, so were easy enough to handle. I concluded (rightly or wrongly) that had been where Declan added most value, the 'back office' mechanics. But when it came to control and ownership... Well, things were much more nuanced.

Remember what I was trying to do. I was still intending to sacrifice myself to the process, to my work, the production of my books; but in parallel I was exploring these new avenues and calculating what the likely rewards were going to be (some defined in the numbers, some not). Allied to all that, I believed I could mould the fictional 'me' to play the role of the interface. The real me would produce the work, the fictional me would be my agent.

- You'd become Declan?

- In a way.

Think of it as a triumvirate where, instead of me being in the minority, I would be holding two of the roles. If you want to talk about symbiosis, then talk about that! The contracts I envisaged were with myself: 'fictional me' landed the deal, then 'real me' delivered the product. A bit schizophrenic I'll grant you, and maybe I didn't rationalise it in that way at the time, nor understand the potential longer-term impacts of doing so. The important thing was to keep control, give nothing up.

And to avoid the carnivores; those within the industry who ate writers up. The Big Apes. The chewing and spitting out. If writers sweat blood for their art (highfalutin, I know!) then my commercial imperative was to turn that metaphorical blood into the most significant amount of money I could. I was prepared to sweat the blood, but I wanted the benefit of a full financial transfusion in return.

- Very 'medical'.

- More Burke and Hare perhaps.

- Macabre.

Throwing myself into the guts of the industry, beginning to dissect the landscape on the flip side of the coin, I soon realised that the method was too ingrained, the format too well-established to be broken. It would be like expecting my volume of stories to 'out-do' Shakespeare. That was never going to happen. It might sit alongside, a companion piece maybe, but it was no usurper.

Realising the overwhelming power of the beast quickly banished the idea of my own press (for want of a better label); the big boys would ride rough-shod over that. So it became more about working with, alongside, collaboratively. You choose the words for a change. From my perspective as a potential solo entity, my quest — and it's romantic to call it that, don't you think?! — quickly became as much a matter of survival as anything else: find a way to circumvent a slug of the process *and* avoid being devoured whilst doing so. It was a little like striving to be a secret agent, working behind enemy lines; or a double agent — with 'agent' being the most appropriate word in the world!

- And Declan?

- What about him?

- How did he take it?

- Not without scepticism.

He heard rumours and so confronted me. Inevitable really — especially in an industry where everyone knows everyone else and no-one keeps their mouth shut. He'd taken the odd phone call: *What's all this about Charles E?* and *Did he know…?* or *Have you been fired?*

All of which led him to raise it with me. We sat in the pub (our usual haunt for 'business meetings') and he asked me what was going on. So I told him. *I'm not looking for a new agent,* I said, *I just thought I'd try and go independent for a while.* His response — *And if that doesn't work?* — gave me the opportunity to leave the door open: *Then I'll come back to you with my tail between my legs.*

Even as I made that commitment, I couldn't foresee any circumstance where I would need to make good on it. Not necessarily because of Declan, but because I was determined to make a go of things on my own.

- Cocky.

- Which is exactly what I knew you'd say.

- Of course you did. How could I say anything else?

- I'd prefer 'confident'.

- Hmmm. I can think of other words beginning with 'c'…

- I didn't know your vocabulary was so extensive.

You could call it rebellion if you'd a mind to. And maybe my decision was as much that as anything else. Whatever; it was still unavoidably predicated on me having something to sell. The 'what next?' question. When I had two or three publishers nibbling, that was what they all wanted to know.

Universally they were supportive of not going back for another bucket-load from the short story well. The general consensus was that whatever came next needed to be career defining, a 'blockbuster' as challenging as *Spoonful*. Wanting to to fanfare my new liaison with them, they would say that wouldn't they? One of them (I forget who) even said *It's time to stop pissing about, Charles*. It was the same story as before, of that there's no doubt — only now there was no-one between me and the source, no-one needing to justify their 15%.

For a while, disheartened by the whole gambit, I returned to the notion of going it totally alone; but I was already frustrated with all the creative time and effort the search process was costing me. If I had to do all the grunt work around marketing, printing, distribution — as well as the writing! — I knew that would drive me insane. I made some enquiries about independent specialists who professed to have the skills and contacts — but when you added all those costs in… To a certain extent it was better the devil you knew. Or one of the devils you knew. And Declan was waiting in the wings. Don't think I couldn't feel my tail heading back toward the space between my legs…

That aside, as we edged towards 1996 the 'what next?' question remained unanswered. History offered some 'blockbuster' nuggets: the end of the Bosnian war; O J Simpson; Philip Lawrence's murder and the rioting that followed; Fred and Rosemary West. Potential there certainly, but not exactly my bag.

And then a chance meeting. In a way a collision between my past, present and future — and enough material to last a lifetime.

Underwear

That day my intention had been to do no more than undertake a reconnaissance mission. Whenever I was in London I liked to try and drop in on Waterstones in Piccadilly; it was a large enough bookshop without being daunting (unlike Foyles!), and sufficiently diverse — in terms of layout and architecture — to be interesting. The first floor mezzanine café, being set out in a 'U' shape, allowed its patrons to sit drinking their tea or coffee whilst looking down onto the book-browsers below. From time to time it was a location which had provided me with the odd idea, a flash of inspiration. Closer to home, I preferred the Nottingham branch; its architecture was more elaborate even if the clientele was entirely provincial.

Given I'd had a prospective-publisher meeting not that far away, Piccadilly seemed like the ideal place for a coffee before I headed back to the Midlands — and it would give me an opportunity to get a sense of how my books were doing.

To be fair to them, Declan and MacMillan had persuaded Waterstones to give some prominence to the Shakespeare collection, the residual evidence of which was a few stray copies residing on a 'buy one, get one half-price' table. Although to the uninitiated being discounted like this might seem commercially detrimental, but these offers are incredibly popular among loyal Waterstones' customers, and so making it to such a table was — to a certain extent — to have 'arrived'. *Spoonful* had never been recognised in such a manner, but nevertheless I found a copy on a shelf elsewhere (not unreasonably between fiction's Ds and Fs), plus my short story collection in their specialist section.

Buoyed by what I considered to be, on the whole, a reasonable representation, I made my way to the stairs in a positive mood. Uncovering such evidence would surely be in my favour when it came to arguing my case with potential

"

new publishers. As it happened, that morning's meeting had gone well enough, but the imprint concerned remained hesitant — which was fine as they weren't my first choice partner anyway.

As I ascended towards the café I became aware of an increased level of what I can only describe as 'murmuring' on the ground floor. Stopping to locate the source, I saw a woman being escorted through the store by a member of staff — and with someone I can only describe as a 'lackey' trailing in her wake. I recognised her instantly and, when she happened to look up to where I had paused on the stairs, there was something in her glance which suggested the recognition was mutual.

Soon established at a table with my coffee, a general turning of heads and a change in the tone of extant conversations forced me to follow the café patrons' general gaze only to find the aforementioned woman (servant still in tow) not only heading into the café, but making a beeline towards me. *Charles*, she said, speaking a little too loudly and from slightly too great a distance, *I thought it was you!* Compelled to do so, I stood, allowed her to plant a kiss on my cheek, at which point she addressed her acolyte — *Roger, get me a latte* — and then promptly sat in the chair opposite mine. Clearly satisfied with her entrance, she smiled in my direction and said *So what brings you to town?*

It was the first time I had ever met her.

Katya Valentine was, in many respects, something of an 'old school' celebrity. Unlike many modern B- or C-listers elevated to notoriety thanks to 'reality' tv and/or a selection of unnaturally sculpted body parts, Katya had worked her way up from a grounding in print journalism before finding a niche in radio. The step into daytime television had been something of an inevitability. When in full war paint, Katya was striking enough, slim enough, and youthful enough to pass for a woman who was still heading towards forty rather than one who had breached that particular dam three years previously. Her beauty, mingled with the persona of being a 'serious' individual, put me in mind of a cross between Elizabeth Taylor and poor Jill Dando, someone else who's star was on the rise at the time. It was no wonder people recognised Katya; no wonder they stared. Under such a combination of circumstances, any association with her — however fleeting — was hardly going to do me any harm.

Here to give that awful Russel Craig another going over? So *that* was how she knew me. I smiled. *Oh, I suspect my television days are over.* She laughed, professionally. *Nonsense! The next time you write something wonderful you must come and talk to me about it on my show; I'd love to have you.* It was professional flirting: a blend of the shallow and the sincere, delivered with sufficient volume to allow her offer to carry beyond our table. Some people were looking our way, but I managed to resist acknowledging them.

Roger returned with her coffee. *Give me fifteen minutes,* she said, then turned towards me again. I had a sense the opening gambit was over.

Although quite obviously extrovert — at least as far as her public personality was concerned — she managed to carry off its display with sufficient élan to prevent it from seeming crass. Indeed, as with the aforementioned Ms. Dando, there was something entirely captivating about her. You couldn't help but be drawn in, within minutes feeling yourself totally and utterly 'on her side'. This was the cocktail which made her such Daytime TV dynamite. And given she had a serious 'edge' about her — the ability to levitate into the highbrow as and when needed — was it any wonder that Katya was one of the most 'eligible' single women in broadcasting? Who wouldn't have liked to have had her on his arm as they walked some red carpet or other? Yet against all the odds, Katya had managed to more or less protect her private life; there was even the unanswered question as to whether 'Katya Valentine' was her real name. The general consensus was not.

There had been red carpets and men on her arms, of course there had; and in a quest to find a story the paparazzi had, on occasion and based on photographs or hearsay, attempted to add one and one, and most often managed to make them add up to three. Some of these were motivated by envy; the absence of hard evidence, something concrete that could be pinned on her, merely serving to make Katya more enticing, more mysterious. She would laugh off suggestions of intimacy when she could — which was most of the time — and had been lauded for one rebuttal when a few years earlier a male television interviewer had asked her if she wasn't ready to settle down and have children: *Why, do you think you're man enough for the job?* she had asked. The audience had loved that — and the interviewer immediately realised that he could *never* be up to the task. As far as she was concerned, when posing questions to others she had a method of delivery which both disarmed the interviewee and simultaneously seemed to hint at many other levels of interrogation besides. The *Here to give that awful Russel Craig another going over?* she bowled me was one such example, and although I'd played it with a straight enough bat, I was immediately conscious of the existence of other subtly implied questions.

- But it was more than that.

- What was?

- Your response.

- How can you say that; you weren't there.

- I'm always there.

Perhaps it was no more than a question of timing. Or serendipity. I'd largely been celibate for a couple of years (by my standards anyway) and so with the two new collections behind me and the decisions about Declan and my immediate publishing future made, it was perhaps inevitable that I felt primed to step back into the emotional trenches. You might argue (if you've been paying attention, that is!) that to take on a 'project' such as Katya represented a major challenge (for the fictional me, of course) but I'd decided — even before she left for her next engagement — that she would be my next amorous target.

- You thought *you* were man enough for the job?

- I think your tone is unacceptable, don't you?

- *My* tone?

Having waived to the waitress in order to get a second coffee, I tried to visualise the wake created by Katya's departure: eddies in the air, along the aisles, between the tables of books. I also wondered if I could define my new objective as specifically as I had my quest for a new publisher. A red carpet or two would probably come into it at some point, plus the promised appearance on her show. Of course, the precursor to both of those would have to be access to her home and her bed.

I confess my ambitions were entirely selfish. Or predatory. 'The thrill of the chase' if you like. Call it 'research' if it helps, but I also wanted to get beneath Katya's veneer (in both senses!) and resolve what made her tick. In addition to finding her instantly fascinating, there was, I suppose, the allure of a potential triumph if I succeeded where other men had tried and apparently failed. First among equals: an ambition which had driven me ever since The Hive, and which had manifested itself most recently with the Shakespeare take-offs. Why shouldn't I see if I could make the still-immature loosely fabricated second version of myself successful in an alternative field of battle? This ambition wasn't akin to my relationship with Hazel in any way; the notion of 'love' never entered into my head — at least not as I sat there drinking coffee. Remember: do something, move on. And up. Answer a question, then pose another. No repeats. I've always hated repeats.

- Yet you're happy to engage in this current repeat…

- This is a new endeavour.

- But the events aren't.

- Maybe they feel new to me. Or this interrogation of them does. And what the fuck would you know about it anyway?

- Nothing. Or everything. I'm just intrigued to find out whether you're going to unwrap the lot.

- You make it sound like a present.

- Isn't it? And wasn't that what Katya was: a present to yourself?

~

There's a kind of autopilot you slip into when you meet someone for the first time. You have to be open and friendly simply because you never know what might come of the connection — after all, everyone has a story. That's even more relevant if the someone is 'known' one way or another. They are immediately valuable to you, have the potential to be useful — though let's face it, they may also do you damage in certain circumstances: a misunderstanding or a mis-placed word; something arising from confusion or a failure to live up to expectations.

I recognised Charles from the show he did with Jessica — and the wonderfully misplaced 'fucker' comment from Russell Craig. It wasn't that I was drawn to him per se, you understand; that wasn't why I followed him up to the café and gave him my "nice to see you!" at full throttle. The event with Jessica, Craig and that other guy made him interesting. Known — or beginning to be known — allied with being interesting is quite the cocktail when you had the kind of show I'd built. If my programme was going to continue to work (i.e. they were going to keep renewing my contract) then I had to ensure I wasn't going over old ground. Interviewing Craig would, for example, have been the very epitome of 'old ground'.

Was there more to it than that? That's the question I'm always asked. The answer is always the same: not in the beginning — and certainly not in those first fifteen minutes drinking coffee in Waterstones, whatever anyone else may say... But after that? Soon enough, I suppose.

In the sense that Charles was interesting, my hunch was right. Given how long I'd been doing my job, the experience I had, I was confident I could get a handle on people — their 'potential' — pretty quickly. Fifteen minutes was twice as long as I'd usually need. And then when, very early on, he made it plain he was taken with me — and not merely as someone he could butter-up in order to try and get on their show — well... I was flattered. And remember, he was interesting.

Maybe it was just an accident of timing; the overall composite making me find him attractive. And why not? I discovered soon enough that he'd a reputation — which should have warned me off I suppose — but that only seemed to make him more enticing. Doesn't everyone have an agenda? Or two?

Of course in the end I found out there were aspects to him I didn't see. I mean, the kind of things you wouldn't want to imagine of anyone...

~

There was one major hurdle to be overcome: *The next time you write something wonderful you must come and talk to me about it on my show.* That's what she'd said, and — flirting aside — what I'd assumed she meant. However, at that point I was writing nothing. Katya was nourished by news, by fresh things; her programme always had at least one musician, writer, artist, or public figure promoting their latest album, book, or show. If I was going to be of interest to her (professionally that is) I needed to have something to feed her. She was savvy enough not to be interested in past glories unless they were relevant in the context of something topical, new and exciting.

'What next?' reared its ugly head again. First Declan and then my potential new publishers. And now — and even more significantly — it was a question I needed to answer for myself, because without doing so I would get nowhere with Katya.

The idea, when it came, was blissfully simple: I would write a novel about a man pursuing a woman who may or may not be out of his league, and who represents something aspirational in terms of his sex- and love-life. And I would write it *in parallel* with my adventure with Katya: 'the public Charles', my superficial persona, would have the experience and then pass it on to 'the writer Charles' who would then take the raw material, manipulate it, and turn it into fiction. It was a notion so aligned with what I was trying to achieve in terms of the fictional me that I almost cried out when it landed! There was such a strong element of symbiosis: my two selves feeding off each other, meeting the desire of always moving forward and undertaking a new challenges — and now one infused with a side order of intimacy. Given my prior romantic entanglements (small 'r', and Hazel notwithstanding) I had sufficient history of my own to give the main character of my new book a credible backstory. My own version of Alfie.

Of course, even though the fiction would be disguised and 'different', at some point in the new work there would need to be a major divergence, that locus where art ceased to imitate life. Exactly when that occurred would be dependent on how things progressed with Katya *and* how much of the romantic wringer I chose to put my hero through. I also knew that at some point I would face the imperative of deciding whether my book's protagonist was going to succeed or fail (irrespective of my own venture) and if the latter, resolve how that failure was to be represented.

If I had already subconsciously decided he would fail, was that to ensure I distanced the narrative from my forthcoming lived experience because I was confident *I* would succeed? I didn't want Katya suspecting an overlap between her reality and my fiction. There was a fine line to be trodden — which was another challenge in itself.

But first I had to open the door, to obtain soundings as to whether I could get both projects off the ground — and one of them depended entirely on Katya. Was I going to have to force a closed door or merely push against the one Katya may have already left ajar? The latter couldn't be evidenced by anything as superfluous as her generally flirty nature, and which I assumed to be nothing more than an essential part of her public self. The one clue she offered was in the last thing she did before leaving the café: she had me unlock my phone so that she could punch her number into my contacts' list. 'Katya xx' was how she'd labelled herself.

Well then.

I messaged her the following day to say how delightful it had been to meet her, that I hoped we would see each other again soon — and that I had a new project in mind and hoped we might discuss it at some point. In her response (which bounced back more rapidly than I had expected) she explained she was going to the States at the end of the week but could make dinner before then. If I was interested.

- 'Interested'?

- Her word, not mine.

- Little did she know.

- You think? From where I sit now I think she knew very well.

- Did you drool over her in the bookshop? Had you been that obvious?

- Not consciously. But 'Katya xx' told me something, as did her invitation.

- Which was?

- That there had been a spark. Those few minutes we had spent in inconsequential conversation had been sufficient. A fuse had been lit.

- Lit fuses almost always lead to explosions…

Her invitation wasn't a trap. I didn't regard it as such then and still don't today. In spite of all the gloss and show, I soon discovered that Katya was actually quite a lonely soul — but oddly one who hated solitude. Over dinner I casually asked her why she had made the invitation, suggesting she surely had other more eligible contenders to spend an evening with. She swished the notion away (though hardly with a 'straight bat'), refusing to be drawn on her romantic status. Most questions I asked she laughed off before turning them back on me, a tactic which allowed me to offer her a sanitised version of my relationship with Hazel — and describe my present romantic situation as "unsatisfactory". That was a word she picked up on and, in doing so, gave me a sign — to quote Sherlock Holmes — that "the game was afoot".

As if to reinforce the point, we met again almost as soon as she was back from America. Within a month our dinners became more discrete, the restaurants less 'showbiz'; quiet little bistros off the beaten track where she knew the proprietors well enough to ensure discretion. About four weeks after Waterstones, and following one of our dinner dates, she invited me back to her house for a nightcap. It was an externally modest — though internally very large — terraced property near Pimlico.

- 'A nightcap'; that old euphemism!

- Yes; except in Katya's case that was all it was — that time.

- You surprise me, a man with your track record.

- I was playing a relatively long game remember — and harvesting experience for *Curtain Call*.

I'd already given it a title. Drafting the opening was going pretty well, certainly well enough for me to offer Katya obscure hints. And as I learned more about her, I was able to embellish my female lead accordingly — though obviously I didn't explain her role in that!

- And you learned about yourself too?

There was a line Katya seemed reluctant to cross. All the while giving me the impression that I was on the verge of winning her over, I also had a sense of her deep-seated concern that I was no more than a typical Romeo hunting the same treasure as all the other men she'd known. And to a degree I was, obviously. So she continued to hold something back, keep a critical part of herself in reserve. She wasn't teasing me exactly, but more than once I left Pimlico with the distinct impression that the odds were increasingly stacked against me, that there was nothing I would be able to do to emerge triumphant. My victories were akin to getting the upper hand in minor skirmishes, nothing more. Most evenings when I saw her, I could later be found a little before midnight attempting to hail a taxi to take me home. Occasionally I made it to breakfast.

My place was somewhere she never visited. We were playing the game entirely on her turf.

- And on her terms, sounds like.

We were jousting, both mentally and physically; that's how I prefer to think of it: the two of us wrestling with each other based on disparate criteria we held close. If she had her own ambitions, her own rules — the motivation for keeping 'secrets' — then so did I. She never knew I was using my experience of her as source material. Of course if she chooses to read this (and she will have her own reasons not to) then all will be revealed — but I suspect we're now both too old to care.

~

It wasn't a question of deliberately resisting — though I can see how it might have been perceived as such. Especially by Charles. Especially with his reputation. Maybe my caution helped stoke the fire. But I'd been damaged enough to be cautious; that's all.

Oh, I'm well aware what the gutter press have said about me over the years, but they've never had the full story. And they aren't going to get it. Any reticence on my part (if that's the kind of word you want to ascribe) had nothing to do with sex — I wasn't frigid, for Christ's sake! — but rather it was a reflection on my need to feel, I don't know, 'comfortable'. Maybe I'd decided quite early on what was going to happen between Charles and I; if so, that made our combustion inevitable. Think about all those dinners we had — and so soon too! That tells you something.

Don't ask me what the trigger was or whether there was one event which persuaded me to let the drawbridge down, that first evening when 'nightcap' meant more than brandy and coffee. Don't ask me because I can't tell you. Maybe it was no more than a sense of 'comfort'. Or a look; the right kind of words spoken; even the lingering touch of a hand.

Nor should you ask me what I'd thought about the future — or even if I had done so. I was bruised, remember; and Charles was carrying all this 'baggage' around with him, his reputation for playing fast-and-loose. Even though I was savvy enough to understand how I might be recognised as 'a conquest' by him, that wasn't how I wanted to be regarded longer term — and I didn't yet know whether Charles 'did' longer-term. Or if either he or I were up to it. Maybe that was a question I'd already started to ask the moment I tapped my telephone number into his phone: 'xx' marks the spot...

~

I liked to imagine that our relationship was running in tandem with what I was trying to do in terms of finding a new publisher, a new modus operandi — after all, the output from one project would feed the other. Or was that true by default, whichever way you looked at it? Other than that, it was a parallel drawn from the perspective of control, of being able to better steer the action. There was no beauty parade involved as far as Katya was concerned (not in the same way as I was trying to get prospective new publishing partners to jump through hoops) but other than that…?

In the end, settling on Picador came about almost entirely because of Hugh Leach. Hugh was my contemporary, born the same year as me.

- Or us…

A solid and pragmatic individual with a decent track record and a quick wit, he seemed to be in the same camp as me in that he regarded the majority of agents as no more than a necessary evil: people who 'ran interference' — or got in the way — and for a cut which, after the first book deal, they never really earned. I asked him about Declan. *One of the better ones* was as far as he'd go. Picador had given Hugh licence to harvest one or two direct clients and — just as importantly — he had read and liked most of my work. *The best is yet to come,* he said the first time I met him, *that much is obvious.* I told him about the draft I'd just started working on, though without the source material's origin. *The plot's neither here nor there,* was his first somewhat dismissive observation. I was reminded of Declan. *Go too far one way and all you've got is 'Mills & Boon'; but go far enough the other way…* I asked him what he meant. *Your lead needs to be dangerous, a bit like Bryson; or incredibly vulnerable, insecure, flawed, doomed. Or there needs to be a twist when it comes to his love interest, something about her the reader isn't expecting. And then how you wrap the whole thing up — <u>that</u> needs to be pure Charles.* I had no doubt about achieving the latter, and told him I would work on the former.

Did his comments influence how I behaved in my relationship with Katya, how I crafted the fictional me? Did it effect which lens I choose to view her through, or how I might have tried to shape events — or even shape myself? Art directing life, and not the other way round? Maybe yes, maybe no. But the fact that Hugh made those observations served to draw those two major threads more tightly together and thus increase the sense in which they were profoundly interdependent. In an odd way it seemed as if I was living my work.

I still wonder whether, for a writer, life can ever get more intense than that.

- But…

- What do you mean, 'but'?

- Isn't there always a 'but' — especially when you wrap something up so nicely. All that symbiosis nonsense.

- It wasn't nonsense.

- And weren't you forgetting one major thing, the potential 'fly in the ointment'?

- You've always been so susceptible to cliché.

- Well?

If there was a reason behind Katya's reticence it was one which could be traced back to a painful experience she'd had in her early twenties having gone 'all in' (her phrase, not mine) with someone she met at the start of her radio career. They turned out to be, shall we say, 'unreliable': already engaged, but still playing the field; looking for short-term satisfaction and, ideally, a short-cut to the top. Initially he'd fallen for Katya because of her looks and personality; back then she didn't have two beans to rub together. However, as far as the gentleman's affections were concerned she was up against two far more promising candidates, one of whom — much older but in a position to call in favours elsewhere — held most of the aces. By all accounts Katya's dumping had been brutal, the villain of the piece soon finding his career catapulted skywards on the back of his wheedling and conniving. Once he had ascended high enough, had found his own wings, he then betrayed his former benefactress too.

Katya didn't tell me who the individual was, largely because he's still in the game; and whilst dishing the dirt would have been appealing to her on one level, she wasn't the vindictive type. What she did tell me, however, was the effect it had on her. Out of circulation for a while, she forced herself to work hard, to face into her heartbreak; she cultivated confrontation with it because that was the only way she felt she could come out the other side, scarred but not beaten. Determined not to make the same mistake twice, she found herself constantly on her guard where men were concerned. She called it 'reinforcing the girdle'; an approach that wasn't as extreme as chastity — but wasn't that far off either.

Do girdles have hoops? I'm no expert. But if there were hoops, Katya was happy enough to make prospective suitors jump through them. A lot of hoops. Maybe that's why, over the years, there were increasing levels of rumour about her love life; none of her entanglements ever seemed to settle and become concrete. Again she shared no names, but I got the distinct impression that the few ambitious souls who had tried to comply with her rules simply gave up.

- And you?

- What about me?

- Did you successfully jump through all her hoops, or did you abandon the field?

My fictional character — the one in *Curtain Call* — crumbles psychologically (my episode of sitting paralysed on the edge of the bed helped again!); and then, having crumbled, decides he wants revenge. But our heroine (if I can call her that) is well prepared. Hence the somewhat gory conclusion. Which Hugh loved by the way. Very commercial.

- I wasn't asking about the book.

- No, I know you weren't.

- Obviously she didn't go after you with a knife, but did you give her cause to?

- No.

Or yes, depending on how you want to look at it.

After a few weeks it seemed all too likely that, in spite of her 'encouragement', I was destined to become another one of the 'nearly men': so far, but no further; so close, but no closer. A remnant. I called on every trick I had in my armoury. And make no mistake, this wasn't just about sex. Or maybe it wasn't about sex at all. No; my ambition had settled itself on something far more complex. Victory was defined as Katya giving herself unconditionally. Sharing of self, I suppose; profoundly. If my initial goal had merely been to have sex with her, as soon as that box was ticked the challenge shape-shifted beyond that. Probably because of the way she locked-up such a large part of herself. Breaking through all her layers became the new quest: to get beyond the superficial and what she was prepared to gift me relatively freely, and then to plunder that which she prized above all else.

- Which was?

- Her self, I suppose.

- And?

- 'And'?

- Or should I say 'but'…

~

The cul-de-sac was tucked away at the very periphery of an estate which would have been the height of fashion when built some twenty-five years previously. Apart from the inevitable weathering, it hadn't changed much since then, and, as a result, it was impossible for him not to feel as if the rest of the world had moved on around it. A short stretch of road with four modest houses on either side soon gave way to what he could only regard as an 'unfinished' crescent: an arc with a span of perhaps forty degrees hosting another six properties along its outer side. Cassie's was the penultimate residence on the left.

He paused at the junction with the arc and endeavoured to take in her property from a distance of around seventy yards. Down to the exposed fake wooden frame, it was pretty much exactly as she had described it to him. In spite of this, he doubted whether the house and the road on which it sat would conform to all he had been expecting — she was, after all, an exceptional woman. But then perhaps a construct as inanimate as a building could only offer up the 'skin deep', an inarticulate shell. Unless one were particularly imaginative or inventive or wealthy, when it came down to it individualism was almost invariably expressed on the inside, in private. In any event, he doubted whether her neighbours would have allowed her to render the exterior of her property purple or yellow — or even render it at all. There were standards to be kept up, a certain uniformity to be adhered to. Nevertheless, he couldn't help but wonder what she might have done to the place had she been permitted. Didn't they say how a dog looked reflected its owner? If so, then why couldn't a house prove some kind of mirror too? Purple? Unlikely. Yellow? Ditto. But some off-white heading towards pink? Perhaps.

It was a contemplation which, other than to prompt a scan through an imagined colour chart, yielded little in the way of insight or conclusion — except to confirm that he didn't yet know her well enough to successfully complete the exercise. Oh, he had the superficial elements certainly — her looks, her shape, and, more recently, how she liked to kiss and be kissed — and although these were enough for him to continue his pursuit, to move on to the next stage of his campaign, he was aware that in themselves such facts were ultimately inadequate. Which, after all, was why he was here: to expand upon his knowledge and experience of her.

As he started walking again — imagining her on the look-out at one arc-facing window or other — he couldn't help but smile at the subtle yet compelling way in which he had managed to engineer this invitation. It was testament to how far he had come with her — and a clue as to how much further he might yet go.

~

Our 'final encounter', as it were, was crudely documented by others for public consumption, falsehoods nowhere near the truth. Largely based on rumour and guesswork, the gutter press choose to fill the void with whatever they felt would sell. Journalists hate a vacuum! To the outside world we simply stopped seeing each other. There was some speculation, a little bizarre and unimaginative dramatisation, but the 'official' line was that we'd run our course. Motives were ascribed; there was an almost pathological desire to find 'fault': she had tired of me; I had tired of her; she had wanted commitment but I had not... Nothing very original there.

For a while afterwards I confess that I was worried Katya might choose to frame our combustion in a different way, something closer to the truth — and publicly too. But she didn't. Perhaps because I had come to know so much about her, sufficient to hold a few trump cards of my own; or perhaps because I had, in fact, succeeded in getting through — emotionally I mean.

I hadn't set out with any specific intent that evening. We'd not seen each other for a couple of weeks (she'd been away) and I was, I suppose, 'up for it'. Isn't it amazing how, just occasionally, where you are in the craft can bleed into real life. The other way round is, of course, the more natural; indeed, isn't that the way inspiration works? Perhaps it was more than coincident that I'd also just reached the end of the story I was drafting. Given I'd just killed off my main character, condemned him to failure, perhaps I was 'heightened'; maybe I was determined *not* to follow in his footsteps. There had to be a division between the outcomes for the fictional him and the fictional me. Here was a circumstance where I couldn't afford for life to imitate art.

- So you ended up with life imitating life.

She said she wasn't 'in the mood'; that she'd been 'thinking about things'. Red flags of course. Warning flags. But to flash red when I was feeling so bullish..? I could tell I was about to be kicked into the long grass exactly as Katya had been all those years before. That was the nub of it. So, if I'd read her correctly (and I was sure I had), then I had one last chance…

- To do what?

- You might well ask.

- I think I just did.

- One last crash through her defences, I suppose. Exert my superiority. Win.

If there was still a way to persuade her not to cast me aside, time wasn't on my side. We were talking for hours — or maybe just minutes. And even though I realised the victory I had been seeking was essentially a mental one — manifested by her 'giving in' on some cerebral or intellectual level — in the remaining time she seemed to have allotted me the only card I had left to play was my physicality. There was suddenly no more 'long game'. Even though I'd no intention of Katya becoming my 'life partner', it was easy to see how my actions could have been interpreted as such. Perhaps that's what scared her off. Irrespective of that, I'd been chasing her a while and it now appeared I'd not managed to make as much progress as I'd hoped…

Look, I'm not proud of what happened — and sometimes I'm not really sure what did. It wasn't as if we hadn't made love a number of times over the previous few weeks. You could look at it from one perspective and call me 'enthusiastic' or 'passionate'. Embracing the last throes. Or if you considered it from another angle… Well, then it might look like something else.

- An echo from history?

Afterwards she threw me out. It was the culmination of our affair, coincident with my arriving at the fag-end of my novel though luckily — and to Katya's credit — I hadn't been stabbed to death with a bread knife.

- She might have been tempted.

- Looking back, I can see that.

Knowing it was over, I told myself she had contributed to the denouement as much as I; that the climax had been more of her design than my own. It's easy to conjure a scenario in which I was Katya's pawn; to spin a tale where — knowing we were finished — she wanted one final intense experience to give her a sign-off with which to remember me. I don't think that's unheard of. A bang and not a whimper, perhaps. And if you consider she was back at work within a couple of days, appearing on a tv-screen-near-you as if nothing bad had happened… Evidence for the defence? You might have regarded her ambivalence as a statement of triumph — and public confirmation of my defeat.

Which I couldn't afford to recognise, of course. Having that as one possible interpretation of our relationship's conclusion (it wasn't 'closure', obviously) I had no alternative other than regard it as the opposite. Indeed, I found myself fired-up enough to immediately plunge into the first edit of *Curtain Call* with a verve I'd never experienced before. When Declan had talked about 'edge' he'd had no idea really. *Now* I found my writing had an edge! Using my final experience with Katya as the touchstone, I was able to infuse something into my prose which made it severe, dangerous. Later a reviewer said *you could cut your fingers turning to the next a page — and even knowing that, still can't help yourself from doing so.*

- And now?

- What do you mean, "and now"?

- How do you view that 'climax' given the distance time has put between you and it? Or between you and her?

We've met a few times over the years. Informally, at one event or another. She never invited me onto her show, and she moved on to explore other avenues soon enough; but our collisions were cordial enough: brief in the main, and unsurprisingly a little 'cool'. I've not spoken to her for years. Perhaps 'professional' is the best way to describe those last few encounters. Professional and insignificant.

- Why 'insignificant'?

- Because the evidence would suggest that I didn't impinge on her career in any way — and I found I didn't need her to progress my own.

~

In my weaker moments I wonder if it was all my fault. Isn't that common enough, especially if — in spite of all contrary appearances — you're not that self-confident an individual? Emotionally, I mean. And maybe a sense of guilt comes with the territory, being a woman. So I ask myself if I might have handled the situation a little differently, found a gentler glide-path out of the relationship.

But in the end there was no glide, just a nose dive.

Was the crisis brought about because we had decided what we wanted the future to look like — and because those visions were radically different? I had a sense that Charles had made up his mind; he seemed particularly charged that evening, as if he wanted to shift things in to a different gear. Had he decided he was in it for the long-haul? Was I to become 'serious', his 'Hazel mark-II' — even if he claimed not to have wanted such an attachment?

I never found out, of course; but maybe it was a sense of that which scared me, especially as I'd decided I was heading in the opposite direction. He seemed to want 'in', and I wanted 'out'. If that resulted in me getting scared then I might have been abrupt, decisive, confrontational even. A mistake, given Charles' track-record. An accelerant; fuel to the flames.

Even so, even if all that is true, it doesn't excuse what happened. Nothing can excuse what happened, what he did. I can't take any responsibility for that. I don't want to take any responsibility for that.

He should have just left. We should have had the argument and that ought to have been it. I wasn't prepared for... How can anyone be prepared...

~

As soon as she opened the front door he could tell there was something different about her — and not merely that her make-up had been applied a little more liberally than usual, the shade of lipstick an edgy intense red. Oddly he recalled his first impression of the house from all those weeks before, the way he had debated with himself the colour of render she might have chosen to apply had she been free to do so. Now as he stood on the threshold he could only imagine it a darker shade of pink.

She had been drinking a little, that was the give-away. He could tell not by her breath when she kissed him welcome (which she did not do) nor by the vaguely haphazard application of her warpaint (which was usually applied impeccably), but rather there was something in her walk, the way she almost 'sashayed' away from him, which suggested a certain looseness. If all that was indicative of anything then it was surely that the evening would be a memorable one.

"White or red?" she asked over her shoulder.

Convention. She knew very well he only drank red. Perhaps she had been sampling both; perhaps her question was further evidence of inebriation.

He chose not to answer, and she walked on as if knowing he wouldn't.

"I've made some garlic bread to start," she said as she reached the kitchen door, pausing to see whether he would follow her or go into the sitting room. "I can bring it through."

When he kept on walking towards her, a slight smile played on her lips, one which only succeeded in exaggerating the redness of her lips against the whiteness of her teeth. He doubted they would make the main course for some considerable time — and even whether they would get to eat the starter. If she had planned to excite him so soon, so immediately, she had surpassed herself.

In the kitchen two pots simmered on the hob, steam rising from the un-lidded one. On the small central island, a large trivet was set out with two pasta bowls alongside it. Beside that, two side plates, a large breadboard and, still wrapped in foil, the garlic baguette awaiting deployment of the large black-handled breadknife which lay nearby.

He paused for a fraction of a second, then moved on again. She edged closer to the island, rested her hands on its surface, breadboard and knife within easy reach.

~

We'd become — what's the word — 'irrelevant' to each other. And especially so when Katya started seeing Michael. He had his own history of course. Being single (for the third time!), handsome, eligible, wealthy, their coming together made sense on a number of levels. He was older than her by just enough to make him both 'safe' and still a 'good catch'. They were a golden couple for a while; small-scale Burton and Taylor. So Michael ended up becoming the one who accompanied her on the red carpets, on whose arm she hung. Presumably agreeing they were too old for children, in fusing their individual parcels of fame they morphed into an item whose the sum was greater than its constituent parts. An eventual marriage made commercial and emotional sense. Even if matrimony was habitual for him, I think I was pleased for her.

- And him?

- I only spoke to him a couple of times.

We moved in vastly different circles. He showed no indication of being aware of my history with Katya. But then he *was* an actor, so…

In a way we were all moving on: Michael to another marriage; Katya to another man and a different kind of relationship — and possibly just the one she needed.

- And you?

- Yes. Me too.

The episode with Katya added another layer to my public persona, the fictional me. It had nothing to do with me the writer or with my craft, but — I don't know — I suppose it elevated my PR. Hugh regarded "all that Katya stuff" as something he could work with. *Most writers are as dull as dishwater* he said, *either that or they're entirely anonymous. But now you've written a new chapter for yourself.* He said I'd made myself "more visible and interesting", and that could only be a good thing when it came to sales.

Which — from one perspective at least — meant that my Katya-related ambitions could be regarded as 'mission accomplished', even if I hadn't been able to fully articulate at the outset what the pragmatic goals were. After all, she helped give me the subject matter for *Curtain Call*, key elements of the plot. And when it came to characterisation, I was able to steal quite liberally both from her and my second self. That proximity meant there was a great deal to do in the first edit to ensure I put sufficient distance between fiction and reality — *to disconnect* was how Hugh put it. But that kind of thing, manipulating truth and lies, was child's play really. It was something I was good at.

- And you?

- What's with this 'and you?' all the time?

- The 'real' Charles, if you want to look at it that way. The man behind the mask. The boy who fell in love with Hazel.

- Older. Wiser. Aren't we always? And, I suppose, ready for the next encounter.

- Now that you were revenged.

- 'Revenged'? How so? And how typical of you to frame it in such a way! Revenge against who, if you don't mind me asking?

- You're the one doing all the talking…

~

Curtain Call? I knew some of the background, of course; Charles offered me a partial picture. How could he have had his affair with Katya and then prevented it from influencing the work — especially when the subject matter was, well, 'aligned'?

Was I interested in the facts? Not really. I was only concerned about the work, the quality of the book, the writing, and what it might do for us (and when I say 'us', I mean both Charles and the business). To a certain extent, Katya was a sideshow. Given how Charles described their split — and the relationship before that — I couldn't really interpret it in any other way; after all, I only had his description to go on, and Curtain Call was fiction. Had I been interested in the truth then I would have needed to go digging, ascribe motive. But that wasn't my game.

And don't forget, it was also none of my business. I'd been presented with this laser-sharp piece of work — brutal, uncompromising, unromantic — and that was all I cared about; my job was to get it out into the world and selling, not concern myself with the origins of the source material. There were rumours (there are always rumours!) and you can choose to lend them some of your time, allow them to deflect you from the task in-hand; but that wasn't my style either — and it wasn't what Charles wanted or needed from me. My role wasn't to be some kind of quack confessor. And let's not forget, Katya hadn't tried to kill him — at least not to the best of my knowledge!

Did he need a confessor anyway? You tell me. When the rumours got ugly for a short while, I did wonder — but once again, that wasn't my bag.

Cows

2001

Some people have suggested I would make a great salesman. They do so based on the assumption that my primary motivation is winning. They choose isolated incidents — usually the more obvious ones with Craig or Harris, Declan or Katya — and apply reductive reasoning, trying to condense events into nuggets which allow them to point out some common constituent element. 'Winning' is what they come up with most often. And I can see why. But such analysis is lazy, leading to comic-book conclusions which merely demonstrate they don't understand me at all. Or maybe even 'life' in general. They pluck at straws, draw erroneous parallels, miss the subtleties. Few recognised the dichotomy, the difference between the public Charles and the private one who does all the writing.

I say 'few'; it may be none.

Of course, there's no harm in admitting that if something stands in my way — either an external entity or one conjured up by me as a challenge — I like to meet it head-on; but surely there's something much more complex in play under those circumstances than merely victory or defeat? It's not like watching your favourite football team or having a bet on the horses, two arena where 'winning' and 'losing' have real meaning and tangible outcomes. What about the subtle, the emotional?

For example, my relationship with Hazel was never about 'winning' — nor, thanks to Millar, losing. Why should that experience be regarded as different to any other young man's addiction to his first love? Or later — and perhaps even before Hazel — I think I can argue that my sexual encounters weren't focussed on being 'victorious' but were rather a finding out about myself, the world, how everything hung together. Or didn't. And then later, unscrambling how I could use what I'd discovered in my work. If you wanted to be truly reductive I'm pretty sure you could take *everything* anyone ever did and locate it in a framework whose sole points of reference were victory and defeat: the fight to achieve the former, defence against the latter. Lazy, like I said.

On the other hand, if you chose to see 'experience' as educative — whatever the outcome — then the landscape you create is an entirely different one, as must be the person moulded by it. Education implies lessons, and lessons imply take-aways, the things you should — or should not — do next time. For there always seems to be a next time. Oh, it may be cloaked slightly differently and come upon you unexpectedly, from left-field as it were, but arrive it will, either stealthily or trumpeting alarums. Everything I ever did — or wrote — informed what I subsequently produced. Lessons. If *Tainted Harvest* was a triumph (i.e. 'winning') then that victory was essentially temporary. I see that now; temporary like most victories. The privilege of wisdom. The most important thing about the play was that it facilitated what came next; without *Tainted Harvest* there could have been no *Sunbathing*. And isn't that how we're supposed to live our lives? Or how writers are supposed to live theirs? Write something half-decent, then write something better; write something decent, then something good. Write something good… You get the point.

- And where are you now?

- I gave up keeping score a long time ago.

- Or that's what you tell yourself.

- Touché.

Curtain Call was another step on the journey, another entry on the CV, brick in the wall, gem in the portfolio. Tick. If someone wants to regard it as merely another 'win' then I can't stop them. Horberry, Harris, the lot of them; all they're really interested in doing is applying a label to something unlabelled — even if it defies labelling. Job done. Whether that's because that's all they're capable of, or all they're asked to do, or what their 'readers' want from them… Well, I leave that up to you.

- And Katya? Another step on the journey?

- If you like. But be careful.

It's easy to be reductive there too, with the women. The notion of 'conquest' can be applied so much more readily when it comes to matters of the heart (whether or not the 'heart' is involved at all). But if you wanted to view her in that context then you'd need to consider Hazel and all the others in the same way, a continuum made up from both serious encounters and the less so. "Steps on the journey"? I suppose so. Notches on the bedpost, or marks on a scale? In a way — but only if you're determined to view me in a specific light.

- Which is?

- As a relatively simple organism, incapable of little more than pandering to base desires.

- But in your defence you're also a writer — or so you claim.

- Yes; though even that can be pared down to nothing other than a flimsy veneer if you were determined enough to do so.

But whether anyone else is prepared to or not, I'm certainly going to give myself kudos for being more than a hack, more than someone driven by 'winning' — even if winning is measured in sales, prizes, awards, accolades. It takes something special to be able to split yourself in two, create a duality in order to combat the monsters, the giants, the dogs you face. And yes, also to understand that the byproduct of all those lessons is the prize of learning. We may not recognise it, but when we start out instruction is most often imposed on us by other people, usually as a fait accompli — even those lessons we unwittingly cull from people like Horberry and Imogen. For fuck's sake, even people like Martha!

But you know who hosts the best lessons? Not others, but ourselves. Those are the most potent, the ones that pack a punch; they can double us up, leave us gasping for breath — and we never forget them. Or should never do so. Like sitting on the edge of a bed for twenty minutes.

- Is that what Katya did, leave you 'gasping for breath'?

- Maybe. Maybe not. It's an interesting question. Even I wrestled with it for a while.

- I'll take that as a win.

- Very funny.

- But you see what I did there? Learning from the master.

- Overall though, I don't think she did.

- And what about me? What did any lessons involving me teach you?

If there's a prize to be had from learning lessons — and I'm talking in general hypothetical terms now, not those associated with 'winning' and 'losing' — then I think it's wisdom. You might even prefer to call it self-knowledge. Which is partly what I meant when I said about not keeping score; I don't feel the need to, not any more — at least not in the way I did with Declan and Hugh. Back then scores were evident in concrete numbers: sales, rankings in paperback charts, the number of four- or five-star reviews. I'm not saying they weren't important. At the time they were vital; after all, you had to have something to navigate by. But later, after *Curtain Call*, came the real dawning, as if a whole raft of lessons had clubbed together, bundled themselves up, and offered me the 'big reveal'.

Namely, that the greatest reward I could hope for from my efforts — 'from' *and* 'for' the real, authentic, writerly me — wasn't to be found in numbers or accolades but in catharsis.

- Sounds a bit 'hippy'. Even disingenuous.

Through variously exploits — including the one with Katya! — I have been able to cross-examine my relationship with Hazel to such an extent that it and I have declared a truce. Writing about it (however tangentially) helped too; there's a great deal to be said for vicarious living. So understanding my 'inclinations' was no longer an itch I needed to scratch. Yet if I traced a line back from Katya, joined all the dots to try and resolve my emotional life as if the whole represented an equation which required solving, I found myself — time and again — arriving at the hard and impenetrable brick wall of Martha O'Connell.

But Martha was different gravy. There had been no exorcism as far as she was concerned. In spite of all my navel-gazing, I came to realise I'd done nothing more than propel her to the back of my mind. Perhaps I assumed my anger would be enough to keep her secure there, penned in. But fury is an ineffective gaoler. If — to give myself a chance to finally defeat her — I didn't release her from the mental cell in which she was kept so that I could have the requisite fight, then how could I ever reconcile myself to what she had done to me?

- To us.

- Yes, us. Obviously.

- And 'reconcile'?

- I suppose I mean come to terms with. Or vanquish. And I know that means accepting the winning-or-losing thing, but in her case…

Hardly a single day went by when she'd not tortured us — either physically or emotionally. She'd been hell-bent on pursuing her own form of 'winning', day in, day out. And beating not just us, but humiliating Timothy too. I don't think I'd ever been able to rationalise the impact of such a foundation until the combustible combination of Katya and

Curtain Call, followed by Hugh's chomping at the bit for something new. And all the while the public Charles was off enjoying himself at dinners and events, at readings and book-signings — primarily for ladies of a certain age, some of whom seemed to regard the denouement of *Curtain Call* as erotic wish-fulfilment. 'Basic Instinct' anyone? And while I'd been off lauding myself, a creative void had been growing within Charles the writer and it was into this cavity Martha unexpectedly burst.

Lessons give you wisdom; that's what I said, didn't I? Well maybe I also understood that any wisdom related to my experience with Martha could never truly be harvested until I finally managed to lay the old bitch to rest. Perhaps it had taken all that time — and all those words written across the decades — in order for me to be suitably armed and armoured. One thing leading to another, remember. Not quite a breadcrumb trail; nowhere near that subtle.

So that became the next holy grail: put Martha O'Connell to the sword. It didn't matter that by then she was already dead; indeed, she'd been dead for nearly ten years or so. But this quest wasn't about her, not in the sense of impact or outcome. 'Personal, not business'; that old cliché swapped round. Even without her physically in the picture, I knew I was still staring into a fight — and a fight I could potentially lose. But the prize! To have her gone. Not locked up in a metaphorical cell, but banished completely. No, banishment is wrong. Executed. I needed to assassinate her, and there was only one way that could happen.

Settled on my goal, I spent a few weeks kicking ideas around, thinking about characters, plot lines. For the first time it felt as if I needed to go into battle fully prepared. Dead she may have been, but I was still wary of Martha's reach; I had no doubt she could do untold damage from beyond the grave. The depth of planning I undertook was unusual for me, my habitual laissez faire completely absent; no flying by the seat of my pants. If you think about what happened with Katya,

I'd made things up as I went along — both in terms of the relationship and *Curtain Call* — but I knew such an approach wouldn't do if I was going to destroy Martha. In a way that made the challenge even more risky: I could fail to destroy her *and* fail in the endeavour *as a writer*. Double jeopardy, you might say. From Hugh's perspective, well, he saw none of that. He liked the idea, it screamed commerciality and would fit incredibly well as a follow-on to *Curtain Call*. More damaged souls; more emotional mayhem. *You seem nervous* he said to me over dinner one evening. I told him 'nervous' was an inadequate word.

- So you had to confront me too.

- You? I don't think 'confront' is the mot juste.

- I wouldn't know. But how could you talk about Martha and what she did to us without including me?

- Don't kid a kidder! You know perfectly well how: I did so by leaving you out.

~

As far as I was concerned A Cold Dish *trumped* Curtain Call. *It was another step up, edging into a different league; proof of what Charles was already capable of — and what he might be capable of in the future. For me, it also cancelled out any negative residual echoes from* Curtain Call, *at least as far as Katya was concerned. I was getting to know how Charles worked, what occupied him and what didn't; and I'd never seen him as focussed as he was those months when he was working on* A Cold Dish. *If he'd been invested in* Curtain Call *because of Katya, then he'd doubled down on a project which, I knew, was the most personal thing he'd ever embarked upon. At least that was my reading of it.*

If you want my technical opinion, he'd kept all the sharp edges and rawness from Curtain Call, *and overlaid it with a different kind of emotion. Oh, there was emotion in* Curtain

Call all right, how could there not be? And if Katya's influence pervaded that narrative, then it couldn't be anything other than personal. But in A Cold Dish *it seemed to me that he'd reached deeper into himself, harvested some darker pain from his past. He had enough to mine, after all.*

I knew some of his story. It was well enough documented here and there; you didn't get to where Charles was — or where he was trying to get to — without having to let some of your history slip. When we were talking about the book (as he was drafting it) occasionally he'd cast a few more details in my direction in response to some query or other. It was like being fed jigsaw pieces one at a time. My habit was to want to understand why a character did what they did, where their motivation had come from; in the case of A Cold Dish *maybe I asked specific questions related to his past simply because I didn't believe people could be so cruel. "You've had it easy, Hugh" he said to me one day. I thought he was being dismissive, some kind of inverse snobbery, but now…? I can see he was probably right.*

The big thing — the really big thing — was that the book was <u>so</u> *commercial. Yes, it was 'literary fiction', but it wasn't airy-fairy; there was enough of a dark side to the narrative to appeal to a wide audience. I remember someone asked me about it once and I told them that it was "a bit like a murder mystery — dark and evil — but without the murder". On reflection it was cleverer than that. Charles had engineered it in such a way that the* <u>reader</u> *ended up being the murderer. No-one wanted Mary to survive.*

~

Although on the one hand the story — *story*, mind — was inspired by real events and real people, what I had in mind was nowhere near autobiographical. Close, but never the full monty. Yes, the Martha character was Irish with all the attributes that had been attendant on our former torturer, and yes, she had a husband who was weak and pathetic; but in my narrative there was only one adopted child. And I made that child a girl. Call it poetic licence, but it seemed to me I could do more damage to Martha — and be less at risk myself — if I could make the victim more vulnerable, suffer more readily. And I was sure (and Hugh agreed) that using a girl would not only achieve this but also make the book super-appealing to his target demographic.

I say 'his target demographic' because I left all that to him; he had the grand plan, I was simply supplying the ammunition.

So I became Jenny, Martha became Mary, and Timothy became Thomas. And I turned up the dial on every emotional scale available to me: the pathos, the pain, the torture. Not that the fictional Mary was worse than Martha — how could she be? — but by making the object of her revenge female, and by making Thomas even more lily-livered, that was how she seemed. I wanted people who read the book to hate her. In the end she was almost Dickensian. I confess that here and there it was a struggle to prevent the whole thing from tipping over into melodrama, but it was modern enough and concrete enough, the ancillary characters and sub-plots real enough, to prevent that from happening. And it was bloody well written. Pared back. A gut-punch on every page.

Of course back then I could have had no idea that sometime later — i.e. now — I would be writing the non-fictional account of virtually the same history. Perhaps if I'd never created Mary and Jenny and Thomas I wouldn't have been able to produce *this*. Or it would have turned out to be something completely different. As always, one thing leads to another, and if there's a break in the chain…

~

"Go and get her."

Thomas was unable not to notice that the usual steeliness in Mary's voice had gone up a notch.

"She's upset. Shouldn't we leave her alone for a while?" It was as far as he felt he could go. He knew what teetering on the brink felt like — as well as the impact of stepping beyond it. There were some mistakes one could only recover from so many times. In Mary's world, that number was impossibly small.

"*She*'s upset?" Here was the tell-tale blend of rage and revenge in Mary's tone, the register she slipped into all too easily like a car with a faulty clutch. "You saw what she did with her dinner, where it went."

The evidence was irrefutable; he had been witness, there could be no denial. She challenged him to take Jenny's side.

"But surely an accident."

"It's not an accident that I'll have to clean up after her; not an accident that the food I spent so long slaving over will have to be thrown in the bin; not an accident that the plate is probably chipped beyond all good use… She knew what she was doing! You saw how she leapt up from the chair, the path her hands took from the table to her eyes. Accident? Ha!"

Thomas looked down at his own hands and where they rested. He tried to judge the distance between his fingers and his plate, plan the trajectory they would take as he leant on the table in order to rise from his seat. He knew he would stand, leave the room, go to Jenny's bedroom and try to persuade the poor girl to come down, apologise and be contrite. And he would do so because that was the lesser of two evils, the other being his wife's entry into the girl's room and closing the door behind her.

~

When *A Cold Dish* won the Whitbread I was flabbergasted — though I tried not to show it. Obviously. The Charles who faced the cameras, who responded to the media and attended the interviews, *he* thought the accolade was deserved. It was, after all, his best work to-date. And when pressed as to any echoes from his own life? *Of course there are some common references,* he may have said, *how could there not be? But I'm not a girl. I'm not Jenny.*

- And did they ask you where I was?

- I can't remember.

It was the pinnacle. Or 'a pinnacle'. Just as *Tainted Harvest* had been, and *Sunbathing*, *Dark Corner* and *Curtain Call*. Like climbing a mountain to admire the view — only to find that a little further up the valley was an even higher mountain, the next peak to be scaled. (I quite like that metaphor; I may use it somewhere…)

So I stopped, paused for breath — the 'oxygen' provided by sales, reviews and the like — all the while knowing I would have to move on. And up.

- And this?

- What about it?

- Are you on your way down now? Back to base camp. Are you going to hang up your crampons and ice axe?

- Haven't we already covered this?

- Have we? If anyone should know it ought to be you…

- This may be the highest peak of them all.

- Only if you're kidding yourself.

And then *A Cold Dish* became something else entirely. Almost a celebrity in its own right.

~

At that point, 2001, the book world had never heard of Oscar Gormley. A failed novelist, by the age of forty (roughly two years before *A Cold Dish* came out) he claimed to have written twelve books. Or I should say, drafts of books. No-one wanted them. He'd spent the best part of fifteen years hawking manuscripts to agents and publishers. At the trial he confessed to being in possession of over a thousand rejection letters and emails. More than one a week. Which said a great deal. If you wanted to be generous you might use that statistic to demonstrate his commitment, determination, perseverance. Inclined in the opposite direction, those rejections are not much more than proof of his incompetence.

Beaten down by systemic failure — either his or that of the industry (Gormley had a view) — he'd chosen to stop at twelve; why put himself through the wringer any more? But then he read *A Cold Dish*. In terms of style and subject matter, he believed it wasn't that far removed from what *he'd* been writing across the previous decade. Bruised by years of being pummelled — and choosing to bypass any considerations of quality and ownership — Gormley came to wonder why the book shouldn't have had *his* name on the cover, why *he* shouldn't be the one with the sales, the accolades, the interviews, the column inches. From there it was a small enough jump for him to persuade himself such approbation was what all *his* hard work had earned, what he deserved. So he decided to steal it. Plain and simple. He figured the book market was so crowded no-one would notice. Where was the risk?

While he worked on his 'version' of *my* book, he also spent time researching how he might be able to publish it himself. With technology developing apace, there had to be a way he could produce copies people would buy. Having said that, even under oath at the trial it remained unclear exactly what his initial ambitions had been. He claimed he merely wanted to have a novel out in the world, something with his name on — never mind that he could take precious little credit for the creative endeavour that lay behind it. In *A Slice of Revenge* he renamed Mary and Thomas, made the husband the tyrant and the wife the weaker vessel. Jenny became Jonathan. The rest of the story he pretty much left alone — except for a sensationalist ending which owed more to *Hamlet* than *A Cold Dish*.

And he might just have got away with it if — for once — he hadn't been successful. Not in the writing you understand (after all, he did very little of that!), but in getting a few people to buy it, to review it. And why wouldn't they? — after all it was essentially a Whitbread prize-winner they were reading. There was enough noise for someone in the business to approach him. All those years of failing to gain traction and suddenly people were knocking on *his* door…

It's easy to say this now, but someone should have spotted the link sooner: his new agent, the new publisher. But they were novices too and maybe seduced by potential dollar signs. By the time serious questions started to be asked — by readers who had read my book first and came to Gormley's second — there were already too many copies in circulation (mainly Gormley's original ebooks) for there not to be a furore. When he discovered the deception, Hugh initially tried the softly-softly approach. If Gormley had seen sense or been advised accordingly, he should have backed down immediately; but he didn't. As soon as he put out some cock-and-bull story about having had the original idea years before — and then compounded that lie by suggesting *I'd* stolen the idea from *him* — well, Hugh went in to overdrive.

He'd known legal eagle Zachary Eastaugh for years. They'd been at Cambridge together; Zachary studied Law, Hugh a humanities degree: History and Art, or European Literature. Some such. But they'd kept in touch. Once or twice Zachary had helped Hugh early on in his career when he'd dropped the ball on a couple of contracts. Now that Zachary was making a name for himself in his own field he didn't need small-scale work in the same way he once had; but Hugh was a friend — and I'd won the Whitbread so was 'a name'. It was a PR opportunity for him; coattails and all that.

We gave Gormley one last chance to retract, withdraw — though to be fair we didn't give him that much time to make up his mind. Crumbling under the pressure, he was already well on his way to being unable to make decisions about anything. *It will be*, Zachary said to Hugh and I over a pint one evening, *a bloodbath. We can't not win. Gormless has already destroyed himself and doesn't even realise it*. We'd taken to calling him 'Gormless'; it seemed appropriate.

It took the judge just two days to find in our favour — but that was long enough for the case to make the news, and for Hugh to set-up interviews, photo opportunities. The whole episode was a shot in the arm for sales too; the kind of boost a book needs after the initial rush has died down, like the pulse you inevitably get from a paperback issue following a reasonably successful hardback. In addition to being a prize-winning writer, I suddenly became someone who had been wronged. There was a sympathy card to be played.

Mind you, in the end all our sympathies — if we were being humane about it — should have been reserved for Gormley. He came to realise what a fool he'd been, see the mistakes he'd made; nevertheless, he kept up the charade for as long as he could, kept digging the hole. Soon after the trial he went missing; they found him a couple of days later wandering about nearly two hundred miles from home. I'm sure he eventually came out of hospital, but I've no idea when. I never bothered to ask.

~

No-one recognised my genius. How could they when the world is flooded with so much second-rate work? Or third rate. Or even worse than that. A Cold Dish was, I guess, second rate at best. If you were being generous. The ideas were okay, but the execution lacked my flare, the talent I had for weaving brilliant narratives.

That was one thing. The other was that it was so like A Slice of Revenge I was stunned. Given he had clearly stolen the story from me, I was confounded as to how he might have done so. If someone had picked up Revenge like I'd asked them to, he would never have been able to write 'his' book. All that circumstantial fabrication about his personal history!

Although it hadn't been optioned there were copies of **Revenge** *out in the world, the copies I'd sent to agents years before telling them that they should recognise it for what it was — what I was — and take up the book. So that must have been how he got hold of the plot and its characters: some agent or other — his presumably — knew another agent (one with a copy of* **Revenge***) and they did some kind of back-handed deal. I have the letters all the agents wrote me, so I know their names. He was fed the plot, changed the names of the characters, weakened the ending.*

And then to get it published first. The audacity! As soon as I got **Revenge** *out — well, it was obvious. <u>Then</u> they took notice. <u>Then</u> the agents started clamouring at my door. What other proof did I need?*

But someone — maybe the same agents who'd been in cahoots before — decided to try and turn truth on its head and suggest that <u>I'd</u> been the thief! They had muscle and money, and they had too much to lose. The court case was them making the most of their corrupting power, using the system to subvert justice.

Stressful? Of course it was stressful. But I fooled them by pretending I wasn't well. As soon as it was clear I couldn't win, that they had everyone on their side — including the judiciary — I played my trump card: I disappeared for a while; feigned illness. They could never vanquish someone who was not only in the right but who had loyal readers on their side. I knew they wouldn't desert me. I knew all I had to do was to bide my time, watch him crash-and-burn when it came to his next second- or third-rate book. I just had to lie low and plan my next move...

Soon you'll see. Soon enough...

~

- So you won.

- Won? Yes, of course. Just as Zachary said we would. We couldn't not win.

- And all those other fights?

- Is that how you see them?

- Craig, Harris, Imogen, Horberry, Katya. Even Hazel. Were those not fights of a kind too?

- You make me sound like a pugilist.

- Aren't you?

I would be lying if I didn't confess to eventually wondering what it had all been for. Not then of course, not in the wake of the Gormley case. And probably not for a few years. Between then and now I suppose — or at least in the wake of Katya and Gormley. I was too wrapped up in 'the machine' to do anything other than play my part.

Isn't it the case that when the exceptional becomes the norm you start to take it for granted? There I was, fulfilling all the ambitions I'd concocted over thirty years earlier: successful writer, recognised, feted, wealthy enough… And I'd won. Oh, I know I've poured scorn on the tired notion of 'winning' and 'losing', but in a way they remain unavoidable bedfellows. My writing life hadn't been all plain sailing — the tired cliché of the 'rollercoaster' perhaps — but on balance… I was in my early fifties, all my books were being reprinted, translated, they were constantly in the shops; in various places theatre groups asked if they could put on *Tainted Harvest* and *Sunbathing*. I even helped with one or two adaptations.

Maybe all that navel-gazing about winning and losing has come to revisit me contemporaneously; maybe it was part of the trigger for this. Perhaps I was destined to return to my theme of judgement — not that it's ever been that far from the

surface of things. Wasn't it only natural that at some point —
as soon as I was comfortable in my new skin — I should take
a step back and think about those I'd come into contact with
along the way? Those who contributed to making me what I'd
become…

- Including me?

Something had been proven. Perhaps that was the critical
thing. In my defence I might choose to claim that 'winning'
wasn't the goal but rather 'proof' the prize: proof that I had
perseverance, persistence. Maybe the only difference between
Gormless and I was that I had talent and he didn't.

Not that I cared. The one thing I never did was to seriously
concern myself with what happened to those I'd left in my
wake. Their lives were up to them. I'm pretty sure Imogen
would have been fine, lived a robust kind of life; Craig and
Harris continued to be who they'd always been.

- And Hazel? Did you ever wonder what happened to her?

- How could I not?

- And me?

- We know what happened to you.

- Do we?

You know, it may have been the exorcism of Martha that
ultimately released me. Not from the point of view of success,
or 'winning', or 'making it', but rather in terms of emotional
freedom. Isn't 'closure' the trendy term? *A Cold Dish* freed me
from her clutches — and in doing so perhaps I started to
realise I no longer needed two different versions of myself. As
the century ticked over, maybe the healing process was
destined to bring 'me-one' and 'me-two' back together; I no
longer needed that kind of protection.

But there was one more fight to be fought.

- Only one?

Fruit

2004 - 2008

They want you to do a film.

Hugh's unexpected words, urgently delivered over the phone rather than in person, was replete with both promise and fog. That he chose to call me rather than arrange a meeting betrayed his excitement. But who were 'they', and what did he mean by 'do'? I didn't even bother to speculate, preferring to ask him outright. *A couple of producers attached to Universal — friends of a friend — think they could make something out of "A Cold Dish". Not exactly as it is, they said; they'd need to 'jazz it up a bit', make it 'more Hollywood'. But they want to know what you think — and if you'd be prepared to collaborate on the screenplay.*

Film. Something I'd never even considered. Cinema was for other people, another industry entirely. I was a writer, that was all. Okay, a pretty good one, but even so… Film? And yet there it suddenly was: another challenge, the next mountain in the range. I asked Hugh what it meant. He went straight to the dollars. *You'll be set for life — especially if the film does well. Put your feet up. Job done.* I protested that the 'job' could never be 'done'. It was the kind of vapid objection I thought I was supposed to make.

Whether or not I meant it, my reaction to *Job done* may not have been entirely genuine; after all there was a part of me that couldn't help but see *A Cold Dish* — the book, I mean — as some kind of ending, the manifestation of a goal reached, a life come full circle and a career brought to a natural conclusion. The Whitbread; the exorcism of Martha; that absurd notion (suggested by who, I can't remember) that I was on the road to becoming some kind of 'treasure'. Who couldn't have been forgiven for thinking that it was *job done*? Time indeed to put your feet up, relax, bask in the glory (however modest).

- But that wasn't your style.

- You noticed.

- How could I not? Charles before everything.

- What's that supposed to mean?

- Your claim about not shying away from a challenge, preferring to try and turn it to your advantage. Or make good your escape.

- Thanks.

- By the way, that wasn't a compliment.

There were attractions, obviously. I hadn't got to where I was without being able to recognise opportunity; and, yes, I liked rising to a challenge too. I'd never really thought about the future in terms of pounds, shillings and pence, but when Hugh started quoting numbers at me — guaranteed *and* potential — well, they were figures which would have turned anyone's head.

And the project was *different*. Perhaps that's what appealed most of all; the chance to turn my hand to something new, to add another string to my bow. Seduced — again — by that insatiable desire to prove myself... And if I didn't agree to the film — and Hollywood! — what did I have to counter it? I'd lived with the 'what next?' question throughout my career. If not asked explicitly by Declan or Hugh (or, in other contexts by Hazel, Imogen, even Katya in her own way), then it was never far from the surface of my own thinking. And if lessons had been continuously learned along the way, maybe there would always be one more awaiting me. As there was one more mountain in the valley. How could there not be?

- But you didn't always learn them, did you?

- What's that supposed to mean?

- That you cherry-picked.

- Don't we all?

- I haven't; not for sixty years…

Of course I could have chosen to ignore the lure of the superficial — that is if I regarded Hollywood and buckets of money as superficial! But if I did, that constant nagging in terms of needing to prove myself, to stand up and face judgement, would remain there demanding to be satisfied in some other way. Maybe that hunger was a legacy from those years with Martha, the persistent need to justify myself.

It would be dishonest of me if, after those initial calls with Hugh — and as my hand was paused over an imagined contract — I didn't admit to thinking 'Oscar'. The Whitbread was great; but an Oscar..! Crowning glory and all that. Bullet-proof. Since Horberry I think I'd always wanted to be bullet-proof. Ever since Martha come to that. Until that telephone conversation with Hugh I'd never regarded writing as something which could clothe me in kevlar, make me indestructible. Who wouldn't want to be indestructible?

- Because I wasn't…

Life didn't work like that. But Hollywood: money, more renown, 'cracking America' as Hugh put it… I knew the project would take me out of my comfort zone, but the prize was potentially life-changing. I was in my mid-fifties, so if not now then when? And if not this, then what?

Soon enough my hand ceased to hover over the page. Ink dried.

~

The disappointments started coming soon enough. Maybe that was partly down to Hugh not explaining clearly enough what 'doing a film' entailed (or him not really knowing);

maybe it was my fault for not reading the contract sufficiently closely — though, in my defence, that's hardly my area of expertise. Or perhaps I had naïvely concocted an image of how the experience would unfold and how I would fit in. If I imagined a temporary abode in California for a few months — all sunshine and swimming pools — could you blame me? Being picked up and taken to 'the lot' every day, sitting alongside the director, making suggestions, tweaking the screenplay — or even writing chunks of the screenplay in the first place. Surely imagining all of that was entirely defensible, because that was what I'd been doing my entire life: creating characters and worlds, fantasising about events.

But it turned out they didn't need me, neither the real Charles nor the fictional one — which may have been just as well if he was on the wane. What they actually wanted was a third Charles, a kind of puppet, a figurehead; someone to occasionally be seen, to be perceived as invested in the project. Maybe they just needed a papier mâché version they could wheel out from time to time. So there was no LA villa, no swimming pool. Instead there were a couple of days in a Hilton Garden Inn, the odd transatlantic phone call. Even if the cheques appeared as expected, the earning of them didn't.

What made matters worse was that they didn't think they needed me for the script either. On my first visit the director (you know who he was!) presented me with the screenplay, a monstrosity that had been cobbled together by three of the studio's hacks. They'd done more than 'jazz it up' and 'make it Hollywood'; they'd ripped the soul out of the story and turned the characters into cardboard cutouts of standard Tinsel Town tropes. Don't get me wrong, I could see how it would make a good film — but not a great one. Nor one which would reflect the source material — *my* source material — in an honest way. I asked Hugh about integrity. He shrugged his shoulders. *Take the money and run*, had been his advice. And what about my reputation? *The people who really matter will have read the book; they'll be fully aware of the majesty of your work — and they'll assume the film is just Hollywood wanking itself off.*

That was certainly an option — not the wanking, but taking the money, remaining quiet, keeping my head down. And I daresay there was a version of me — a younger version — who might have done just that. If *he* had been offered a bundle of cash to allow someone to bugger about with *Sunbathing* then he'd probably have told them to fill their boots — and gambolled all the way to the bank. But I wasn't that person any longer. And I wasn't that desperate. *I don't need Hollywood* I said to Hugh about five weeks into the project. The look he gave me was only semi-inscrutable.

What are my options? I asked him. It was a throwback to the question I'd asked Declan all those years before in relation to Craig and Harris. Should I have been surprised that his answers were pretty much the same? Time changes some things very little. *Apart from keeping your head down?* Hugh replayed the approach he clearly favoured. I nodded. *Try persuasion. Or take them on, make a noise. Persuasion's unlikely to work for two reasons: one, you're not American; and two, in their eyes you're essentially a nobody. No offence. It would be different if you were an American 'treasure'; then you could do them some damage.* I could see he wasn't wrong. *I assume,* I said, *that if I tried to 'take them on' then the same arguments about nationality and so forth would apply.* He smiled. *No question. Which means you couldn't take them on, not personally. You'd need someone to act on your behalf. An American; someone who knew how the system worked, where the soft spots were — and where the bodies were buried. Someone Universal would be wary of.*

I asked him if he knew anyone. *I know people who might know people who could unsettle them...* And I couldn't help but imagine the gateway to such individuals would be Zachary.

To this day I've no real idea how Hugh managed to wrangle introductions to Daniel Tiernan and Brody Forrest, nor how Zachary (assuming it had been him) had succeeded to get the latter interested. *There will be a 'consideration'*, Hugh said. I asked him if I could afford it. *If it works out, you could afford anything.* Hyperbole, but I knew what he meant.

As a combination they ticked all the boxes. If I was going to try and apply some leverage, these were the kind of guys I needed on my team. Although British, Tiernan was a bona fide legend; a true 'national treasure' with a string of screenplay successes to his name. And the Oscars to go with them. Up to that point I'd never met him; how easy is it to get one-on-one with a literary Titan? The closest I'd come was being about a thousand tables away at the Whitbread Awards' event. There had been a rumour he was going to present the prizes, but he didn't.

Tiernan had attained a five-star version of the nirvana Hugh had dangled before me: he didn't need any more money, didn't need to write another word, was able to live off the royalties from his former glories. *These days I just scribble the odd thing now and again*, he said when we first met, *just to keep my eye in.* Although feted by movie moguls and courted by producers, Tiernan had a healthy disrespect for Hollywood. *It's nothing personal*, he said, *but I hate having to face the challenge of trying to sift the honesty from the bullshit.* I explained my predicament, that I felt my work was being compromised, and that I had no recourse to push back. He'd smiled. The story was not an unusual one; he recognised it from his first dealings with the industry. *They march to a different drum, I'm afraid: the sound of the dollar.*

And then he apologised, said he couldn't really get involved. *But* — and here he backtracked — *I do have some friends, some influence. I could have a word or two on your behalf; in the background, as it were. After all, it's the least I could do to help out a fellow Brit. And I liked "A Cold Dish".* Even now I've no idea what surprised me most, that he was happy to lobby on my behalf or that he'd read my book.

~

Over the years I've been asked that many times of course. In the early days — when I was still making my way — I used to be only too happy to help: anything to get my name on the cover of a book, front or back, I didn't mind. But later (and by 'later' I suppose I mean the last thirty or forty years) I've not needed to prostitute myself in that way. As the requests have grown, so I've allowed the acceptances to dwindle. Some think money makes all the difference; that a quote like "'Wonderful' - Daniel Tiernan" comes with a price tag attached. That may be a game others play (and too many others I fear) but not yours truly. I don't need the money, and most often the book concerned isn't 'wonderful' at all.

Charles E.? Was he so very different? Was his work 'wonderful'? What I'd read, I liked — so that was a start. And remember, they hadn't asked me to endorse a book. This wasn't about promotion or profile or sales, it was about principle.

I could tell you a few stories about the West Coast! If you've kept up-to-date with my career — my 'cinematic adventures' — then you may know some of them already. Sometimes bruising encounters, sometimes entirely up-lifting. These days? More tedium than anything else. But I won't bore you with the sordid details; that's not what you're after.

It helped that Zachary was in the picture. I knew and trusted him. Well, as much as anyone can trust a lawyer! Only joking... But more than that I was lured by the thought of a Brit suffering at the hands of those American movie sharks. I knew how the industry worked, and therefore what might befall him. It could end up not being pretty.

In any event, I wasn't going to wade in. Not my style. And they had Forrest for that. I knew him too. So I had a quiet word in one or two ears; the sorts of ears that are attached to mouths which have a subtle and influential way about them. It was a tactic which may or may not have yielded fruit, but Charles seemed to think I'd helped.

~

Forrest was as far in the opposite camp from Tiernan as could be. A loud-ish, brash-ish American for whom nothing was impossible. As a lawyer he'd been "working" Hollywood for years, and — this was key — he was not a fan of Universal. *Mind you, they're all the same: whatever it takes to earn the most dollars for the smallest investment. There's a kind of 'golden ratio' — at least that's what I call it. More than 4:1 is good; better than 8:1 is great!* Before he decided whether or not to get involved, he said I needed to be clear what I wanted. That was relatively easy. I wanted a film that was truer to the book and the people in it. I wasn't asking for a complete re-write or for the film to be one-hundred percent like my novel, but there were episodes, characters and characteristics — I outlined them for him — that felt like red lines. *It makes it easier that you're not after a bigger cut. And we like red lines,* Forrest said. *Everyone understands a red line — especially when they choose to cross it.*

Having met them both, Hugh and I got together. *They're primed and I'm ready to press the button* he said. *I just want you to be sure.* I knew the game plan, the outcomes with which I would be satisfied — and I knew what their contributions would cost me, the 'consideration'. Expensive — at least on Forrest's part — but worth it. I downed my pint. *Press the button, Hugh.*

- You could still have kept your head down; taken the money and run.

- Don't think it didn't cross my mind.

- So?

- So what?

- Why didn't you?

- Maybe I was suffering from a dose of artistic integrity, or of wanting justice.

- Bit late for that isn't it?

- Meaning?

- Oh, nothing… Just that you love your metaphors.

Daniel Tiernan was as good as his word: he didn't want money. Mind you, that wasn't the same as not wanting anything. *I've got myself involved in a few side-shows* he said over dinner a little way into our association; *you know, the odd newspaper column, magazine article, even — and don't ask me how I got into this! — 'a podcast'. At least that's what I think they call it.* He was being disingenuous of course, playing up to the image of someone past their sell-by, the kind of 'luvvie' everyone adored. *When I need a break it's often hard to get a stand-in, you know? Can be 'tricky' to find someone suitable. But I've read some of your work, and now that we've met… I wondered if I could use you to sub for me once in a while.* It was impossible to say 'no' — partly because it was Daniel making the suggestion, but also (and primarily) because it would do my profile and reputation no harm at all. Hugh nearly wet himself when I told him the news. "Free publicity" was what he called it.

Yet it wasn't free. It was work — and another stepping outside my comfort zone. Not the writing parts so much, but the podcast. That was a whole new world. I had to bring the public Charles out of semi-retirement in order to get through it. I sat in on a couple of episodes when Daniel was recording them, then co-hosted one session with him — all in accordance with his script, of course! Then he announced he was off to the Bahamas for a month and left me with two episodes of his show to host, one magazine article to write, and three newspaper columns to draft. Whether the owners of those channels were comfortable with my stepping into the great man's shoes I've no idea; the closest I came to knowing was when one of them confessed *this isn't the first time he's dropped someone on us.* If I was unhappy with the terminology they used, I kept it to myself.

I found out later that Daniel had done his Hollywood-lobbying from some beachfront villa just outside Nassau. As far as his involvement was concerned, this was win-win: he got a break from work he didn't need to be doing, and I had him whispering in one or two Californian ears on my behalf.

~

And later? Once Charles was back on the straight-and-narrow? I'd grown to quite like him, so it was never really the case of me thinking he 'owed me'. If he thought that, well, I couldn't really stop him could I? When I had the idea about the articles and the podcast, that seemed so perfect: I would get some time off and be released from what was fast becoming a chore, and he would get more exposure. It would help his career. Maybe his association with me didn't do him any harm. I'm not saying his work was exceptional, though. Brilliant in places, certainly; but here and there, less so. And some of it wasn't quite to my taste. But that didn't matter. He was good enough, keen enough; seemed a nice enough person. Oh, I was aware of some of the stories about his private life (particularly with Katya who I also knew having been on her show a couple of times in the dim and distant) but there was nothing in his legacy that could taint me. His business, not mine. So we built up this kind of 'arrangement'. And friendship too, I suppose. I know he's referred to me as 'a friend' and I'm not going to disabuse anyone over that...

~

It would have been against Forrest's nature for him to work in such a subtle manner. He took one pass at the production company when he played nice, and then, given that got him nowhere, bypassed the next four chapters of the graduated 'play nice' playbook and brought out the 'big red button'. He made it perfectly plain that he was prepared to push it: I'd withdraw my approval for the film and make it very public why I had done so. It also helped that he'd found a couple of loopholes in the contract I'd signed. He gave them a week to think about it.

Luckily we weren't that far through shooting; had we been, I suspect the production company might not have been so accommodating. *"See you in court" will always be one of their options* Forrest said when we were initially discussing tactics and deciding how hard to play my hand; *but it won't be their preferred choice. If they choose to go down that route then <u>you've</u> already lost — at least in one sense — but they also know they can still lose out too.* I didn't bother to ask him in what sense I might lose. It was the only time during the whole process I had my doubts.

They came back with a suggested list of changes. I countered. There was an all-day meeting between the producer, director, two of their writers, plus Forrest and I, at which details were discussed, compromises agreed to; the rest of that week — *and* the one after — I spent working with them on some rewrites. It was the only time I got a villa and a pool!

- And it was worth it?

- Depends how you measure worth. Or success. But overall? Yes; I'd say so.

There was never an Oscar, of course — nor should there have been, in my humble opinion. But at least the film didn't tank; it did well enough at the box office (the returns ratio was 'good' but not 'great') and most of the reviews were positive. The lead actors and director were complimentary. On release there was a great deal of bonhomie at the launch party. People talked the film up, and for a short while I had hopes… Then Forrest said *Everyone talks up every movie. It's part of the pantomime. The film could be bullshit and at the launch party still lauded as a Cannes certainty.* I've not seen him since then but for no reason other than our paths haven't crossed. According to Hugh even though Forrest's just turned seventy he's still plying his trade troubleshooting in Tinsel Town, gold-plating the name he's already made for himself. And presumably upping his fees. A villa with a pool — or multiple villas — would simply not be an issue for Forrest!

Which was unlike Tiernan. He was seventy-three when I met him and already putting the breaks on. His working on the podcast stopped not long after the film came out, and he gradually cut down his 'side-shows'. Now in his nineties, he spends most of his time in Nassau, writes the occasional article, judges the odd competition; he recently joked that he's starting to describe himself as "Venerable Guest Judge". When invited — and if he's in the mood — he'll grace the odd talk show, both here and in the States.

He and I do keep in touch though. I took over his podcast for about nine months when he gave it up, and the odd invitation still lands on my doormat which, I'm convinced, arrives as a result of him making a suggestion, putting in a good word — or turning down something he can't be bothered with. He denies it of course. I only hope I'm as generous as he is when I get to be his age.

If I get to be his age.

- I'll ask again: was it worth it?

- If you were trying to be dispassionate, objective…

There was a great deal gained from those three or four years: the whole Hollywood experience; my profile growth in the US; an increase in sales; the friendship (if I'm allowed to call it that) with Tiernan — and the offshoots from that, like the podcast and so forth. And then there was the money. Hugh was right: the bank manager was happy; I could afford to put my feet up and slip down a gear…

So if you chose those to be your measures of worth then the answer's pretty conclusive; I wouldn't need to be vigorously cross-examined nor submit myself to a lie-detector test for you to reach a verdict.

- But those weren't your measures?

- I'm not saying that.

Then soon enough Hugh was coming back at me with "what next?" And I had no idea; none at all. It wasn't that I was played out, nothing could be further from the truth; but there was little I could get excited about. For the rest of the noughties I didn't write much or do much — other than Tiernan's podcast for a while. It wasn't that it didn't matter any more; but it felt as if I'd reached a point (I'd turned sixty) where I should take stock — and I had the opportunity to do so. Maybe the notion to write something like this — a 'bookend' if you like — first came to me around then. Was that when the seeds were sown? After all, there was a great deal to look back on, to process, to pass judgement on. And not just passing judgement on me. There was quite a supporting cast list, all the way back to my mother…

- *Our* mother.

Martha, Imogen, Hazel, Craig, Katya, etcetera. And the peripheral characters too, like all those vaguely anonymous women who helped fill the voids that followed Hazel and later Katya — because in her own way Katya created a void too. Did I have a sense that I needed to do justice to them? Maybe. But if so then it was largely an intellectual, unemotional assessment. Occasionally I wrote about them almost explicitly; it seemed as good a way as any to arrive at a conclusion. I began to build up a little collection of short stories, tales of people who were begging to be absolved — or found guilty. The scales of justice.

Was I weighing all those characters for my own edification: 'guilty' or 'innocent', 'winning' or 'losing'? And what about the public version of me I'd created? Or even that brief abomination, the Hollywood one? We were all probably destined to end up in the dock, even if I didn't see it that way at the time.

- And fifteen years on, how do you see yourself now?

- In what context?

- Come on, brother mine; you know the context.

- If so, then you also know the answer.

Underworld

2018

There comes a point where perspective is forced on you. Or it was on me. I wonder if that's the same for everyone; the moment where the rules change for the final time and the components of your life get thrown into the air and you've no control over where they come to earth.

Maybe everyone goes through some version of that, whether it's the falling into or out of a relationship, the hiatus associated with career, or a stroke of bad luck. Or more than one of those. And to various extremes too. I once met a man at a book signing (apparently a 'big fan') who confessed that, aged fifty five, he had never left home. He wanted me to dedicate the book to his mother. I wondered whether he'd ever had any of those pivotal moments where his life might have turned a number of different ways? Sliding doors. Or had he spent all his years — the adult portion of them at least — studiously avoiding such choices? I don't think I ever considered whether or not I envied him. You'll know the answer anyway.

Someone else (it may well have been Tiernan) jokingly referred to a man's sixties as 'sniper's alley' — that period in a life when you're most susceptible to the ailments that are likely to do for you: stroke, heart attack, cancer. Even early-stage dementia. "Always someone else's problem"; isn't that how we try to navigate through those perilous years in order to distance ourselves from the possibility that it might just be our turn?

It was twenty-eighteen and, at sixty-nine, I'd nearly made it through 'sniper's alley' unscathed — that is until my annual check-up with Henderson. Never particularly health-conscious, I'd started seeing Lucan Henderson at the local Bupa hospital when I turned sixty. Now being able to afford to — and with Tiernan's warning ringing in my ears — it seemed to make sense. Clean bill of health and all that.

It's probably not serious he said having just unplugged me from the ECG monitor, *but there's something not quite right. And when I say it's not serious, what I mean is that it's not serious now.* Not the best way to deliver bad news, you might argue. Indeed, I was — and am — reminded of a joke about someone's mother falling off a roof and how badly that news was delivered. At least I think it was the mother. Or maybe it was a cat. I've never been much good at remembering jokes. Anyway, Lucan's rural Scottish roots lent him a style which was simultaneously charming and blunt. Had I the time (and the inclination) I could do something with a character like that. Bryson he wasn't. He thought I'd been harbouring my 'atrial issue' for some time — though less than a year because he was convinced he'd have picked up on it at my previous check-up. I asked about remediation. *There are usually options…*

It's fair to say that I'd let myself go somewhat. An offshoot of Hollywood's money? Or of finally 'arriving' and needing to conform to some updated image I'd cultivated for myself? Too many dinners, too much port, brandy and whisky. Not enough exercise. Bugger it, not even enough sex! Bodily functions had started to become unreliable; I became florid too easily. And although not related, I was reminded that Billy Connolly once joked "never trust a fart!" I've never much liked the word atrophy — and to be fair to Henderson, he didn't use it — but he did say that there came a point where the risks of surgical intervention might outweigh the rewards. *Medication can work wonders these days*, he said. Wonders, yes; miracles, no. He advised me to take a look at my lifestyle: *or the wolves will be at the door before you know it*. I said I didn't tend to have a problem with wolves — at least not the ones I could see…

- Life catching up with you?

- Doesn't it catch up with all of us?

- Some sooner than it should…

Inevitably I translated Henderson's words as light guidance, precautionary, neither a sentence nor an instruction. I tried to take a step back and see what I might be able to moderate in order to keep the good doctor happy — because oddly enough my first instinct was to satisfy him rather than protect myself. And anyway, don't we tend to think of ourselves as invincible, immortal?

- I wouldn't know.

And if I'd already begun to think about some kind of personal retrospective (though not an autobiography, remember) then Henderson merely added fuel to that particular fire. I watched the shadows from my past dance before my eyes like some grotesque freak-show or a Punch & Judy flickering on the wall as if thrown by flames prancing in the grate. "That's the way to do it!" But then you know what happens to Punch, don't you?

It sounds a little self-indulgent I know — or a tad self-obsessed — but more than once in twenty-eighteen, Henderson's recent warning still fresh, I found myself sitting in my library and staring at the bookcase where I kept pristine copies of my work. Just above them, framed on the wall, was the poster they made for the film; and to the side, slightly more dog-eared, the smaller scale and far less professional university posters for *Tainted Harvest* and *Sunbathing* — though to be honest, those didn't really qualify as 'posters'.

And I found myself asking the kind of pointless questions I guess one is fated to ask at such moments: for example, would I have given up writing *Tainted Harvest* for another year of unblemished health? I seemed to be trying to solve another equation based on the assumption that what I had written had an associated physical cost i.e. the 'health' I had needed to 'spend' in order to produce it. Irrational I know, but once I had that in my head — the notion that 'X' words = 'Y' months or 'A' chapters = 'B' years — it simply wouldn't leave me alone. And then, of its own accord, the equation became more complicated — quadratic even — and extended itself to people: what, for example, was the 'cost' of Hazel or Katya in terms of my priceless little ticker? Affairs of the heart indeed! I'd always assumed that living life to the full would elongate one's allotted span; but what if that wasn't the case? All those conflicts, challenges, decisions… The ultimate irony: you only find out when it's too late.

- How far back did your contemplations take you?

- Only all the way.

~

Whether or not someone suffers such moments of hubris, there comes a dawning where you realise you *aren't* actually immortal — unless, that is, your end is early, sudden and unexpected, and beats you to the punch.

- Tell me about it.

Given Henderson's bleak assessment, could I be forgiven if — during the weeks that followed — I might have wished for an abrupt termination? If there was no way out, then why not get it over and done with? Maybe lots of people debate that. A few will act on it.

Yet wasn't I the lucky one? Didn't my work stand for something, guarantee something? Even if I was no longer around, *it* would still exist, and therefore — by extension — so would I. There was a part of me that wanted to have the debate with Tiernan: a grown-up discussion on mortality and what it meant, and how our work fitted into that picture, what role it played, whether it could defeat death. All that. But over the years Tiernan had become something of an existentialist — and a reclusive one too. I wasn't any the less fond of him for that, but it meant I knew which side he would be taking if ever we debated the meaning — or meaninglessness — of life. Denied such an outlet, maybe that's one of the reasons I carried on writing the odd short story, placing characters in climactic scenarios, gifting them different philosophies, and all to examine how things could turn out. In the practical sense the denouement was always the same of course (unless I slipped into fantasy); whether an individual was changed by the process became what I was interested in.

Let me publish them Hugh said. *They're profound and mature pieces; they deserve to be read.* Although not so confident, I was still vain enough to be easily persuaded, and for the first part of twenty-nineteen we were back on the publication merry-go-round. It was distracting, but nothing fundamental altered. I didn't ask what Tiernan thought of the collection, or even if he'd read it. If he had, his response might well have been "so what?"

And then, mid-Covid, I found out that Hazel had been struck down. I can't recall how I knew or who told me, but it was a shock nonetheless; the kind of jolt that forces you to go into yourself, to peel back the layers of your history — each layer a person — and take stock. It wasn't that I didn't know how many people I'd lost, but explicitly facing up to the absence of those who had given my life meaning and provided my way-markers, shook me. That rude awakening might also have had the effect of forcing me to consider them all at once. In many respects we are formed by our interactions with others; they each contribute a slice of our imagined immortality or a layer of varnish (but not the type of varnish that can actually protect us). And then suddenly they're not there… Valerie, Martha, Tim, Hazel, Valerie, Jack, Whitehurst, Hamer, Imogen, Horberry, Millar, Declan, Craig, Harris: all gone. If they each played their part in my construction, did their absence — and thus inability to provide a reference point, an anchor — mean I was in danger of unravelling, becoming 'unmade'?

- And me?

- Yes, Matty; you too.

- Did I unravel you?

- More than anyone.

- Which makes me what?

- Difficult. Problematic. The one who casts the longest shadow.

- And why is that?

- You know why.

- But don't you think now's the time to face up to it? If not now, when?

Leaving the party, Alan got in the passenger seat alongside Hamer, not me. I was in the back with Matty. And I was sitting behind Hamer. When we hit the water it was instantly obvious what was going to happen. Stefan hadn't been wearing a seat belt, so he'd already been knocked out by the car's careening against the arch. He might even have been dead by the time we ended up in the canal.

Things happened so quickly. How could they not? I saw Alan get his door open and, with the water already threatening to engulf me, I knew I had to get out too. Was it luck I managed to get my seatbelt undone before Matthew? Possibly. But how would you describe my panic-stricken clambering over him, using all my strength to force myself to the door first, wrestling to climb out and throw myself into the canal? Self-preservation? Instinct? Wouldn't we all do the same? If there's any consolation surely it's that under such extreme circumstances nothing we do is calculated, considered. I hadn't planned on getting in the car in the first place; I hadn't expected there to be a crash; I never imagined there would be a life-or-death scenario.

Nor did I imagine that, in my blind panic to save myself, I might have condemned my brother.

- You should have let me get out first.

- I know that. I've known it for over fifty years.

- I'd just got my belt undone when you started thrashing about. Was it the force of an arm or a knee that knocked me out?

- ...

- That's why I slipped down into the water. And when the door subsequently closed...

- ...

- You didn't even come back to try and rescue me.

- I did. I swear I did. But it was too late.

- Isn't it always too late? And not just for me.

~

This wasn't meant to be a confessional. Far from it. Yet how can it not be? And what is a confession anyway: the sharing of a secret; the acknowledgement of wrong-doing; the admitting to mistakes? And when engaged in sharing or acknowledging or admitting, each and every reply starts with 'I'...

There is always an outcome (tangible or not) to self-examination, the weighing up of 'a life'. Yet I remain adamant that this 'memoir' is *not* a biography; a biography is comprised of something entirely different. Even if the skeleton is the same, the skin one drapes over a biography is fabricated from some alternative material. There is also the complication of distance and perspective. Tiernan has just published his autobiography. Of course it's largely fiction masquerading as truth, shot through with philosophy. But his life is not my life, his story is not my story, so any comparison is invalid. Drawing parallels is a parlous and ultimately futile endeavour.

But if this 'memoir' is not biography — and if we assume it's not necessarily fiction — then what is it?

- Setting the record straight?

- You're thinking about yourself again.

- No. *You* are thinking about *me* again.

- Touché.

But how 'straight' is that record? If you are offering up a narrative you know will be judged, isn't there an unavoidable inclination to try to weigh the odds in your favour — even just a little? Maybe we go through life doing that, loading the dice, hedging our bets. If I stop and consider how stories might be re-told — not only relating to Matty, but to Martha and Katya too — what does that imply as far as perspective is concerned? How can you pass judgement on me or hand down a commensurate sentence if you can't be certain as to what actually happened? All you have is my reality; or my version of reality; or even a made-up tale told by the fictional version of me punctuated with extracts of my work and the input of others, real or imagined. Does it make any difference to know that, when I set out, I didn't intend to frame this endeavour, my story, in any particular way? That's one of things I've always admired about Molly Bloom's monologue: not only is it unfiltered, it's *honest*, filled with integrity. And it's uniquely *hers*. But then, having settled — gloriously — on that premise and accepted that what we've been told is the truth of a life, for a reader to then be reminded that the whole thing is a fiction and that Joyce has already been fucking with us for five hundred pages…

On that basis — and if you regard this history through a similar lens — then I'm afraid I can't help you, either to know what's true or to assist your arriving at a judgement (if that's where you're heading). Christ knows, I can't even help myself! "Forgive me Father for I have sinned…"

I *have* sinned and I *have* written. Maybe those are the only two things of which you can be certain — irrespective of the veracity of this present endeavour, this battle of wills between fact and fiction.

Perhaps the only option left — from your perspective at least — is to boil it down to the facts ('it' being my life); to gather only the incontrovertible, the proven, those matters of record. Would that help you to, I don't know, do whatever it is you've set yourself the challenge of doing? Passing judgement?

But what would those facts provide you with? Little more than a series of dates and places: born here on this date; moved there on this date. Etcetera. Etcetera. Not a word of dialogue, unless it happened to be captured on film, recorded for the radio. My Whitbread acceptance speech, perhaps, or the skit with Craig and Harris. And if, by navigating my life in such a way, you felt you were scraping the bottom of the barrel too soon, then you will also have realised just how shallow that barrel is.

When we first look at the back calendar of our lives we see acres of white space — which is obviously emotionally unacceptable, disappointing. We want our lives to feel full, worthy, worthwhile. So we go searching for events, things we can tag with start- and end-dates, gems to insert into our posthumous little diary: the date we were reintroduced to our mother; the date of the accident; the first night of *Tainted Harvest*; the combative interview on Jessica's show. And if we can't be one-hundred percent certain whether it was the fourth or fifth or sixth of a month, then we just pick a number. Who cares? No-one. But that's the easy stuff, surface material — like skimming a stone across a lake and thinking we've 'interacted' with it, or can 'appreciate' it somehow. Is four bounces 'victory', assertion of our superiority? Or six? Or eight? Yet the bulk of the lake, the heart of it, is out of sight in the depths we can't reach. Or can't reach *and* survive. "Welcome to my existential world" Tiernan might say.

A few years ago I realised that my name — or its abbreviated version, 'Charles E.' — is actually an anagram of 'Heracles'. Had you spotted that? He was mythological too. What put me in mind of him? Joyce probably; Bloom and Daedalus and Molly, Odysseus and Penelope. (I have a track record there after all…) People regard Heracles' life in terms of his labours; they lend structure, compartmentalisation. A 'bite-sized' life. So if I thought "why not?" can you blame me? Now how do you judge me? Are you swayed either way by the fact that I chose to relate my human-scale journeying in similar episodes, adventures, challenges? Does it make the truth of what I've said any less true? Or more so?

Just like anything else, how we depict a life plays to the fact-versus-fiction dichotomy, our struggle to filter out the lies. If you chose to do so, perhaps you might imagine my own fact-versus-fiction as if it were the set of *Tainted Harvest*: two stories and two different perspectives, each one discrete from the other thanks to a largely intact dividing wall. Perhaps, at various points, you might curate sympathies on either side — from where you sit you should certainly be able to see both.

I don't know.

But my life wasn't like Heracles' of course; there were no kings defining quests, no fierce beasts to be conquered — only metaphorical ones. And Heracles was 'a hero'. No need to ask Matthew how highly I score on that scale.

~

Inadvertently Henderson introduced me to the ultimate beast; somehow ironic don't you think, given his role is to mend, heal, extend life. "Meet Cerberus, guardian of the Underworld. In your case Cerberus is manifested in the form of a somewhat dicky heart." Not that he would have phrased it like that, of course. I'm not sure mythology would be quite Henderson's thing.

Heracles knew that last battle was one he wasn't going to win. As do I. But that doesn't stop the fight; doesn't stop us clinging to that fragile belief — even now that it's no more than an impossible dream — that we're immortal.

So for the last six years or so Henderson and I have been engaged in the struggle, trying to fend off the dog. Or tilting at windmills, Henderson my Sancho Panza. Occasionally there has been a minor victory, a reprieve, a 'buying of time' — as if you could pop down the High Street and exchange your OAP bus tokens for an extra few weeks. Or trade in your pills.

Snipers' Alley? More like a continual running of the gauntlet, the hound snapping at our heels. And even when you're out of the alley (i.e. you make it to seventy) nothing changes. It's all a con. The snipers are always there, no matter how old you are.

Just ask Matty.

Mythology

2024

I now hear Cerberus howling in my sleep. Though not a lullaby (how could it ever be that?!) it has become strangely comforting. Perhaps merely in the fact that I can hear anything at all…

Oh, its echoes become a little more faint each day. Imperceptibly so. And isn't it odd that its homophone — 'feint' — should mean 'to deceive'? Fact and fiction. I could write about that.

Once upon a time I did so. Once upon a time I could have written about anything. But no longer. *Welcome to the club* old Tiernan said to me the other day. It was hard to hear him over the phone, his voice now rasping and fractured; but I know what he meant. Or he knew what I meant. *Race you!* he said mischievously, and tried a dry laugh.

I told him we were both winners — or losers. He could choose. Then again maybe it's innocent or guilty.

Not our choice at all.

~

Did you know that Heracles met Ulysses in Hades? I want to imagine it a kind of 'Old Boys' Club'.

Who else might be there? Daedalus and Bloom? Molly? Even Joyce himself?

And who have I to look forward to seeing again? I could draw up a list.

But I have no control over that either.

Somewhere a dog howls — then is silent.